CINNAMON

BRENDA BARRETT

"Hello," he said.

"Hello," Cinnamon said, hating the breathlessness overtaking her voice.

"I was waiting for you to secure the table for us so I could get my meal and then join you."

"Er," Cinnamon swallowed, "do we know each other?"

"I doubt it. I would remember seeing you before." He smiled. "My name is Jaxon Wilde."

"Oh," Cinnamon stammered, "I've heard of you. Well, your buildings, the grand opening of your latest one was all over the news."

He smiled. "And what's your name?"

"Cinnamon Cooper," she cleared her throat.

"Cinnamon is my favorite spice," he said, "don't go anywhere; I am going to get my food, and we can chat."

She nodded obediently.

Her eyes connected with his for a moment, creating a jolt in her central nervous system. So this was what it felt like—attraction.

It had eluded her for twenty-four years of her life. And today, like a bolt out of the blue, it was here. Her nerve endings were twinging and twanging with it.

ALSO BY BRENDA BARRETT

FULL CIRCLE
NEW BEGINNINGS
THE PREACHER AND THE PROSTITUTE
AFTER THE END
THE EMPTY HAMMOCK
THE PULL OF FREEDOM
REBOUND SERIES
THREE RIVERS SERIES
NEW SONG SERIES
BANCROFT SERIES
MAGNOLIA SISTERS SERIES
SCARLETT SERIES
WILEY BROTHERS SERIES
PRYCE SISTERS SERIES
THE JACKSONS SERIES
CRIMSON HILL SERIES
SPICE AND STONE SERIES
RIDGEVIEW SERIES

ABOUT THE AUTHOR

Brenda Barrett is an award-winning and bestselling author who has a passion for writing real Jamaican romances.

When she's not weaving words that transport readers to exotic locales, you can find her nurturing her green thumb in the garden or doting on her beloved cats.

With an infectious zest for life, this author brings a unique perspective to her writing that is both relatable and thought-provoking.

Don't be surprised if you find yourself lost in the pages of her latest work, as she seamlessly blends romance with some drama, mystery, and suspense, or even sci-fi, leaving readers wanting more.

You can connect with Brenda online at:
Brenalbar.com
Twitter.com/AuthorWriterBB
Facebook.com/AuthorBrendaBarrett

Chapter One

Cinnamon entered the hairdressing parlor and spa where her sister worked and tried to sit unobtrusively in the stylish waiting room. She would probably wait for Cayenne for a while; it was a little after five, and they had agreed to meet at five-thirty. It was her birthday, and they were going to celebrate, but she didn't mind the wait.

The waiting area was like a hotel lounge; the chairs were comfortable, the smell there was amazing and soft jazz music played in the background, creating a serene atmosphere. She would flip through some magazines, see the latest hair trends and spa treatments, and covertly watch the customers come and go. You had to have money to afford Lookbook Hair and Spa's services.

They were a full-service beauty place owned and operated by Tony Ray, who was famous as a stylist to local celebrities and a few international ones. After being on her own for two years, her sister had been over the moon happy to get her own station at this particular salon. She made more money here, met many influential people, and was usually the first to hear when juicy stories broke nationally.

Unfortunately for them, their mother, Anise Crystal, was dominating the current news cycle again. Even today's local newspapers, displayed on the magazine rack beside her, had as the headline: "Former Escort Anise Crystal says she deserves every penny she inherited from the late Senator Richard Greystone. His wife, Noreen Greystone, says not so fast!"

Cinnamon read the first couple of paragraphs:

The war between the late Richard Greystone's family, owners of the Caribbean's leading wine company, Greystone Wines, and Anise Crystal, known for her relationships with high-profile men and who had in the past dabbled with prostitution, has escalated. Noreen Greystone, determined to protect her family's legacy and the reputation of Greystone Wines, hastily organized a press conference at the vineyard estate. Standing before a backdrop adorned with the vineyard's iconic spice and stone logo, she addressed the media with poise and frustration.

"As the wife of the late Senator Richard Greystone and co-owner of Greystone Wines, I was blindsided by my husband's will. I am not disputing how he wanted to disburse his personal wealth; it was his to do with as he pleased. But leaving shares in our family business to Anise Crystal is a slap in the face to everything we've built together," Noreen declared, her voice unwavering. "Greystone Wines has been a labor of love, a testament to the dedication and passion that our family has poured into it for generations. To see it potentially tainted by associations that run contrary to the values we hold dear is both distressing and unacceptable.

"The family's legal team will be challenging the validity of the contested bequest. We vow to protect the interests of Greystone Wines and its stakeholders, ensuring that the vineyard will continue to thrive with the same excellence it has always been known for."

In the meantime, Anise Crystal has responded to Noreen's press conference with a sly wink and her signature sultry smile.

"Richard has his reasons for giving me equal shares as his sons in the family business. I intend to honor his generosity by accepting those shares. I have run a business selling wigs for years; it is reputable and profitable. I resent the inferences that Noreen Greystone is making about me, that I am somehow not worthy.

"I say, bring on the lawyers, grandma. I have my own lawyers, too."

Cinnamon grimaced. She didn't need to read further. At that point, Anise was taunting the family.

Admittedly, it was all salacious and juicy; speculations ran rife as to why the Senator would leave most of his personal wealth to a non-family member and, worst of all, to Anise, a woman who had admitted publicly to doing sex work when she was barely in her teenage years.

That, too, had been a recent interview where Anise had told snippets of her life story, stuff that Cinnamon and her sisters hadn't heard before.

"I did sex work at the tender age of thirteen. I needed to do it to survive after I ran away from home. It was a dark time in my life. No child should ever have to do that. I had customers who many would regard as standard bearers in this society. Let me tell you, there are freaks all over society, and you should not put anyone on a pedestal."

That interview had coincided with Richard Greystone's

death and revelation of the contents of his will. And suddenly, there were all sorts of theories floating around town. The chief one was that Richard Greystone had been a customer of Anise when she was a child prostitute and had left her his money and shares in his wine company to assuage his guilty conscience.

His reputation was taking a posthumous beating in the public sphere. His three sons and their children were catching heat for some of the speculations floating around. They couldn't grieve in peace. For some sections of society, they were guilty by association.

Everyone was shell-shocked, including her.

Her mother's story had always been fodder for local gossip. Anise had lived quite a fascinating life. She had run away from home at twelve years old, got pregnant at thirteen for a mystery man, and refused to share his name with anyone, including Cinnamon, the result of that pregnancy.

She had married Paul Aubry, the famous sculptor, at eighteen and became his muse. She made the news when she found out that Paul was molesting the two children they had together. She had almost killed him; luckily, her aim was bad, and the bullet intended for his head had missed by a few inches.

According to the news, Paul had run out of their upscale neighborhood with Anise screeching behind him, "Not my babies! Not my babies! I will kill you!"

Neighbors had to intervene, taking the gun from her, which by that time had run out of bullets.

There were also her public breakups with a succession of high-profile men. After every breakup, Anise's pictures would be plastered across the papers, social media, and the internet. And that's where Cinnamon had a problem.

She looked exactly like her mother. And if someone didn't

know that she was Cinnamon Cooper, an accountant at Moretti Bedding Company, they would assume she was the woman in the pictures.

Granted, Anise wore loads of makeup and various colored wigs, but the resemblance was there, nevertheless. Looking at Anise was like seeing herself in costume.

That was why she didn't wear makeup or wigs or dress suggestively. That would make her Anise Crystal's clone. It was eerie how much she resembled her mother. She saw her face staring back at her from newspapers everywhere she went.

They had the same almond-shaped eyes, the same dark caramel-hued skin, the same thick curly hair, the same pouty lips, and cute little upturned nose. They had the same body shape, way of laughing, and hand gestures. Her great-grandmother, Sadie Murphy, who she had lived with until age twelve, used to say, "Anise gave birth to herself when she had you."

And it was true.

They were nothing alike in temperament or personality, though. Where her mother was outgoing and the life of the party, Cinnamon preferred to be in the background. She liked quieter pursuits.

But they looked alike, and that was enough. Whenever the various scandals involving her mother broke out, and she was pushed into the limelight, that uncanny resemblance would haunt Cinnamon. Luckily, her sisters looked nothing like Anise, so they passed under the radar quite fine. This burden was hers to bear alone.

Currently, Cinnamon was living like a hermit because of the resemblance. Since the latest will fiasco, she was practically living in fear that someone with a keen eye would look at the pictures of Anise and ask, "Isn't this you in heavy makeup and a wig?"

She didn't date because of that reason. If a guy knew who her mother was, inevitably, he would start to mix the two of them in his head and assume that she had the same good-time girl persona her mother portrayed to the public. There would be certain sexual expectations of her, and it happened like clockwork. She was fed up with it.

One lecturer in her final year of college had asked her to go into the parking lot with him after class; he had actually said he would pay her. That was at the height of another of her mother's scandals when she had a blow-up with her famous boyfriend, and he had called her a glorified whore. The papers had run with that for weeks, and her lecturer had trouble separating her from the storyline.

She had reported the lecturer, of course. The university gave him a slap on the wrist and completely sided with him, basically calling her a liar. She hadn't dated since then. She had put herself under house arrest; her life was boring with a capital "B," and she was not altogether sorry about it.

Until she found someone worthy of getting hot and bothered about, who saw her as an individual and not a piece of meat or judged her based on her mother's colorful reputation, she would be quite happy not to put herself out there.

Most people would not believe if she told them that she had never kissed a guy. She had never been moved before. Ironically, Anise had drummed that into her head into her late teens.

"Do not get intimate with someone unless you really want to. Don't let society force you into thinking that everyone is doing it. Set your own pace, girlie! If you never want to do it, don't. If you feel like doing it, come and talk to me about birth control because I will not be a grandmother in my early thirties!"

Cinnamon smiled at the irony. Anise's mother, Rosemary, had become a grandmother in her thirties.

It was her twenty-fifth birthday, and she couldn't help but feel far behind developmentally.

She didn't want her twenties to pass her by while she cowered in a corner, afraid to show her face. Maybe she should move to another country; she had studied international accounting with that in mind.

While she was thinking, some women had come in, chatting and laughing, carefree and happy. One of them was getting married soon, and they were there to have a group massage and makeovers. They giggled when one of them joked about bikini waxes, and Cinnamon watched them enviously. They looked to be her age.

It was nice to have girlfriends who you were at ease with, to help you with your wedding, and to share jokes with. Her two closest friends were overachievers; Nafia and Ella were too busy to hang out these days. Nafia was doing her doctorate and working full-time as a lecturer. Ella was doing her law degree and recently had a baby.

Ella was the reason Cinnamon was working at Moretti Bedding; her boyfriend, Marco Moretti, owned the company. His lone accountant, Sheila, had been perishing from all the work and needed help.

Ella had suggested Marco hire her, and while she had been grateful for the job so soon after college, she hadn't needed to send out resumes and beat the pavement like her peers, but she was usually swamped with work. Moretti Bedding still needed at least two other accountants, at least someone to deal with payroll exclusively. And Marco was thinking of expanding. At this point, she was so busy she may never have a meet-up with her friends again.

At least she had her sister Cayenne. The three-bedroom townhouse had belonged to their grandmother, Rosemary, but for some unknown reason, when Cinnamon turned eighteen, she had handed her the key and the deed to the property and told her, "This is yours. You can continue to rent it or go on your own, whatever you desire. I know you want to escape living with Anise."

Cinnamon had opted to escape, as her grandmother had so succinctly put it. Being on her own would be no different than living with Anise in her penthouse apartment decorated in unrelieved pink.

Cayenne and Sage joined her shortly after that; they were fourteen and twelve at the time, so she acted as her sisters' mother for a few years.

Sage was still at Mount Faith, a university in the hills; it was far enough from Kingston and bad influences. Sage had gone through a rebellious stage that had worried them all.

It was a relief that she had passed her external exams and had gotten into college. The college was far enough from the Kingston environment to give her a reset.

"You weren't waiting long, were you?" Cayenne pushed her head around the waiting room corner and winked at her. "Why so glum, girl? It's your birthday. We're gonna party like it's your birthday."

Her sister was always a bundle of sunshine. Born with a sunny personality and unmatched enthusiasm for life. It shone from her face.

Her hazel eyes were always dancing with joy; they tended to be greener in certain lights. Cayenne looked more like her father, Paul Aubrey. She had his coloring—light skin and green hazel eyes—but she had inherited their mother's height and modelesque build. All three of them had inherited that from Anise. This month, Cayenne was rocking blonde braids that hit her somewhere near her hips.

She was pretty and sweet and lovable. Cinnamon's heart melted when she saw her; bless Cayenne for wanting to celebrate her birthday.

"Happy birthday, Cinnamon," Tasha, one of the hairdressers, came around the corner. The rest of the people in the waiting room wished her a happy birthday, too, so much for being unobtrusive. Cinnamon grinned and tried to bear it.

"Come on, girl," her sister said brightly. "Let's get cracking. I have a surprise for you." Cinnamon got up and sighed. She hated surprises.

"Okay, so remember last week when I was on the phone with Alex, and she squealed out loudly, and you asked me what was wrong with her?"

"Yes," Cinnamon nodded.

Cayenne and her bestie, Alexandria, were always on the phone, squealing about something; they acted like they were still in high school when they were talking with each other.

"The reason she was squealing was, drum roll, please," Cayenne said eagerly.

Cinnamon looked at her and said without enthusiasm, "Drumroll."

"You are supposed to make a sound, not say it," Cayenne said, "anyway, my customer, Devina Shae, used to be a model…"

Cinnamon groaned.

"She was hosting her fifth perfume launch party at her mansion in the hills and gave me two invites. I would have taken Alex, but it's your birthday, so you get to go instead. I cannot abandon you on your birthday."

Cinnamon stifled a sigh. She had a new accounting system to navigate on her own so it had been a rough day at work and the middle of the week.

Going to a party was not her kind of scene. Enjoying a three-course meal at her favorite Italian restaurant, Bud and Sally's, would have been nice, though. It was just around the corner from the townhouse. She would start with their signature Caprese salad, with fresh tomatoes, mozzarella, and basil drizzled with balsamic glaze. After the Caprese salad, she'd go for their homemade spinach and ricotta ravioli. She'd finish off with their Nutella-flavored gelato.

"Your lack of enthusiasm is telling," Cayenne said as she opened her car door.

"I was thinking Bud and Sally's," Cinnamon said. "I can literally smell the aroma of garlic and herbs wafting through their kitchen right now, and it's close to the townhouse."

"But we can go to Bud and Sally's anytime. Tonight, I want us to dress up and rub shoulders with the bougie. Who knows, maybe you might meet someone you like. I'm getting concerned about you."

Cinnamon rolled her eyes and got in the car. Cayenne just voiced her number one fear. Was something seriously wrong with her? Where was her sex drive, her attraction to others? Not even a spark was lit with anyone since her late teens.

"Maybe something is wrong with me," Cinnamon said out loud.

Cayenne laughed. "I refuse to believe that. There is someone for everyone; maybe you haven't found your someone yet. When you do, you won't be able to contain yourself. I can't wait to see it. Maybe he is at this party."

"Maybe he is at Bud and Sally's," Cinnamon countered.

"Oh really," Cayenne laughed, "we've been going to Bud and Sally's for four years; have you ever seen anyone there to stir your interest?"

"No," Cinnamon said.

"Aren't you more likely to find someone at an uptown party put on by Devina Shae, one of the most connected hostesses this side of Jamaica?"

"I am not looking for someone," Cinnamon said. "And I am not in the party mood."

"The way you live is unhealthy," Cayenne snorted, "you go from work to home, and you don't socialize on the weekends."

"Because I have my mother's face," Cinnamon said.

"And it's a beautiful face," Cayenne said, "the resemblance is not as glaring as you think. Anise's true face is covered underneath a pound of makeup and her various wigs. You are much prettier than she is; you look far more natural and less world-weary. You need to show off that face. You, my dear sister, are going to live your life too. You will have a wonderful birthday night at this uptown party, even if I have to force you to have fun."

"Okay already," Cinnamon huffed, "but we are not staying past ten o'clock. I have a hard day's work tomorrow; it's payroll time, and the senior accountant refuses to use the new software, so it's all down to me. I mean it, Cayenne, not a minute past ten."

Chapter Two

Jaxon Wilde stood in the shadows beside a potted ficus tree with a drink in his hand. He was bored out of his mind. His mother had invited him to her fourth—or was it fifth? — perfume launch. He had forgotten which number it was, but it made her happy when he showed his support for one of these ventures, so he had done her bidding. He couldn't say no. He was happy that she was returning to life, throwing parties, and working the social scene; she was even dating again. Her newest fiancé, Nelson Greystone, was sticking close to her, his hand casually splayed on her half-naked back.

Jax didn't know how he felt about that. The Greystones were family friends; Nelson's children were a part of his life in some capacity or the other. He was best friends with Leo, Nelson's oldest child, and for a few years, he had been engaged to and lived with Carissa, Nelson's daughter.

Currently, Nelson was a potential investor in what would

be his dream villa concept on ten miles of white sand beach in St. Mary. It would be expensive, and Jax needed the backing of rich investors like Nelson.

It would be a drop in the bucket for Nelson. He was one of the richest men in Jamaica; his personal net worth was impressive, and that was without his recently deceased father's wealth added to it. But he hadn't signed yet. When he signed, everybody would want to hop on.

Jax grimaced. A lot was riding on this latest venture, and Jax was weary of the many overlapping lines between him and Nelson Greystone. Anything could make Nelson pull away on the personal front.

If he married his mother, there would be an added blurry layer between business and the personal.

And maybe not; Nelson had not batted an eyelid when he heard Jax and Carissa were no longer together.

"You would have made a fine son-in-law," Nelson had said regretfully. "But Carissa said it was her choice to leave, and I know how that feels. When your mother broke up with me, I thought the world had ended."

Jax had politely smiled through the story, silently wishing he wasn't as ambitious, and needed Nelson Greystone's money to make his dreams happen.

His fingers were crossed, the relationship between him and Devina will work this time. Nelson was single again after his second wife Sandrea had divorced him nearly a year ago, and his mother was single again after husband number three, Williard Wentworth, had a sudden heart attack and died.

No doubt Nelson had ceased his chance to rekindle their romance. They had been high school sweethearts. But had gone their separate ways when his mother met Darren Wilde and fell head over heels in love with the actor who had been the heartthrob in his day.

Nelson had licked his wounds and finally moved on and married someone, too, but through the years, he had made it clear that Devina Shae had been his one true love.

His mother never made any statements like that. She fell in and out of love as easily as she changed her shoes.

After divorcing her second husband, Lorenzo Moretti, she had been giddily in love with her third husband, Williard Wentworth. Williard had seemed to love her just as much. He had been devoted, even going so far as overzealously upping his exercise regime to impress his younger wife. Unfortunately, that had contributed to his demise; he had a heart attack at the gym.

Devina had grieved at his passing, and six months later, she was in love again. Nelson probably thought he had finally hit the jackpot.

She was still beautiful and youthful looking at fifty-five. People were usually taken aback when she introduced him as her eldest son. She usually had to clarify that she had him in her twenties with her first husband, Darren Wilde, the famous actor.

His parents had married quite young and divorced a few years later. He had lived with his father's parents while Devina had flitted around the globe, first as a model and then as the face of her perfume company.

When she moved back home after a few years of living abroad, she returned with a new Italian husband, Lorenzo Moretti, and a baby son, Marco.

It had taken Jaxon years to get over his resentment of the usurpers. He had even grown attached to Lorenzo, who stuck around for twelve years, long after their marriage had died, and then he left and went back to Italy. Jax had been devastated by that divorce.

"When I marry, it will be forever," he had promised himself fiercely. He didn't want to make the same mistakes as his mother; he didn't want to put any child of his through the revolving door of different partners that had been his life while his mother sought love and companionship.

He took things slow. Maybe too slow? Carissa certainly thought so. They had been together for five years and lived together for two, and he had not been particularly moved to take things to the next level.

"I knew I would find you over here, hiding in the shadows," Marco walked over to him.

"Hey, little brother," Jax murmured. "Why are you stalking me?"

"Because I sent you an email, and you haven't responded," Marco said. "You were the one who said I should send you a comprehensive proposal and you would get back to me. I am still waiting; I deserve peace of mind to know whether you will invest."

"I will invest in your expansion," Jax said. "I'll have my secretary send over a more thorough response. I'll pay you a visit tomorrow and glance over the books. That's your only warning of my coming."

Marco grunted. "It's fine; I have good accountants."

"You do know how I normally do things, don't you? I will spend three or more months at your office and bring my team. We stick around and make sure that everything is in tip-top shape, and then I leave one of my trusted lieutenants on your staff."

"Yes!" Marco said excitedly. "Anything you say, anything you want."

Jax sighed inwardly. What was he doing with shares in a bedding company?

He was mainly a property investor; he only gave special

attention to companies he was interested in, which were usually linked to the construction industry.

This would be a sacrifice on his part, but one he would willingly do for Marco, who had taken over the business from his father and wanted to make it bigger and better than how he got it.

He had intended to spend two months off the grid at his cabin in the Blue Mountains for a well-needed vacation after the major headache that was his latest investment—the Wilde Building in New Kingston. It was a multi-purpose residential complex that had all the amenities and functionality of a luxury hotel.

He usually rested himself after high-octane big projects like that. But Marco needed help, and this was his area of expertise. He invested in small companies, helped them to grow, and kept some shares. He hadn't made any losses to date.

"I am going to take a picture or two with Ma, and then I am going to sleep over here in my old room," Marco said tiredly. "I was up all of last night with Noah; he is teething. Ella is studying for her bar exams, and I was babysitting."

Jax chuckled. "Why don't you two hire a babysitter?"

"She called in sick," Marco sighed. "Ella said all this is a part of parenting, and I should deal."

Jax laughed. "I didn't think you two would still be together, and now you have a kid together. Make sure you stick it out for Noah's sake."

"I know, I tell myself that every day," Marco sighed, "but I don't know… there is this girl at work. I can't get her out of my mind…"

Jax frowned at his brother fiercely.

"I know, she is off-limits. It's just that I am young; I am just twenty-six. I never lost my sight when I moved in with

Ella. You lived with Carissa; were you a hundred percent faithful?"

"Yes," Jax nodded. "Carissa and I had a pact. If either of us wanted to cheat, we would end it."

"I can't make a pact like that with Ella; she'd kill me," Marco said wearily. "Anyway, gotta go; I feel woozy. I need a bed, stat."

He walked away unsteadily.

Jax scowled. Thanks a lot, little brother, for bringing up Carissa.

He was certain she would show up tonight. She was his mother's publicist; she had started her own business a few years ago and was working hard to make a go of it.

He wondered idly if he would be moved if he saw her tonight. It would be his first time seeing her since she left their apartment. She had called it quits three months ago after two years of them living together.

"I'm in love with someone else," she had walked into the living room with her bags packed. "As agreed, we tell each other if something like this should happen, so I would like to end it with you before I move in with him."

She had kissed him on his brow and left.

Her abrupt departure from his home and his life had hurt, admittedly. He wondered who she would bring as her date tonight. From what he had heard through the grapevine, she and the guy she had left him for hadn't made it past a month. His attention was fixed on the entrance to the pool area, hoping to get a glimpse of her.

He moved further into the shadows, leaned on the balustrade, and placed his drink on the wall. And then he saw a vision of beauty.

She was wearing a black sheath dress which hugged her modest curves.

Her hair was curly and long, in a side part; she wore bright red lipstick that emphasized her generous lips, and she had a killer shape.

He straightened up from the wall; a shaft of awareness ran through his body. Instant hot attraction swamped him, flooded his system, and made him slightly dizzy.

He had never in his life experienced that before. It was as if everything in his life up to now had just fallen into place.

He needed to know who she was. He felt a tap on his shoulder.

"Hey." It was Carissa.

He had been so focused on the girl he hadn't seen her come in.

"Hey," he dragged his eyes reluctantly from the beautiful girl, gave Carissa a half smile, and then fixed his attention back to the girl.

"What a warm welcome," Carissa declared. "I guess you haven't forgiven me for walking out on you?"

"Huh?" He dragged his attention from the girl and back to Carissa.

"You are punishing me. You are still mad that I left."

"Actually, no," he managed a smile. "You are forgiven. Life goes on."

"Leo said you haven't found anyone else," Carissa pouted, displeased with his flippancy.

"I don't tell my best friend all my business."

"Well, I believed him because you take your time where relationships are concerned. You always take things slow. It took you five years to propose. And then, when we were living together for two years, not a word about marriage."

"You didn't mention it either," Jax said absently. "You were busy with your business, and I with mine. There was no space for a wedding in all of that."

"I heard the Wilde Building is up and running."

"It is," Jax nodded. "I moved in a month ago."

"I am currently single, moved on from Fabian, and I can take a breather from the business these days; it is doing well."

Jax grunted. He wondered why Carissa was telling him that. The girl was in a group chatting. She was probably from one of the modeling agencies. His mother usually hired girls who wore her perfume to mingle with the guests.

It's such a pity he didn't date models. He had a distinct bias against them. His mother had been a model for years and, at that time, had abandoned him to do her job. He didn't need a shrink to point out why he stayed far from models in his dating life.

Maybe he would take a chance on this model. His attraction to her was that potent. He grabbed his drink, "See you around, Carissa," he said. "I'm sorry to hear about the demise of your most recent relationship and glad to hear about the success of your business. You know I have always wished you well."

Carissa snorted. "I could come back, renegotiate that wedding that we never got around to discussing."

"Maybe we never got around to it because neither of us loved each other. It was so easy for you to leave, and it was so easy for me to forget you."

He left her and beelined straight for the girl who was heading for the food station. Maybe he should find them a seat.

Chapter Three

For the first ten minutes since she arrived, Cinnamon felt as if she was being watched, as though the weight of the person's gaze had settled heavily on her body. She kept looking around.

Cayenne grinned. "Do you see what I am seeing? There are cute guys everywhere. Let's go mingle."

"You go mingle," Cinnamon smiled. "I'm heading for the food station."

Cayenne nodded. "I'll meet you up, but if I see you talking to any eligible bachelor, I'll keep my distance." She melted into the crowd.

Cinnamon got a large plate and made her way to the food station, her belly making weird, empty noises. She was pleased to see it wasn't finger food but real serving sizes. They even had menu options from Bud and Sally's. It was a sign she was at the right place. She smiled at the ridiculous thought.

She got the regular selections she usually got at the restaurant, then a few she hadn't tried. She looked around for an empty table but here was none.

And then her eye caught a guy who was beckoning her over. He was standing behind a chair, well above average height. He was classically handsome, the kind of guy that was worth a second look.

In fact, he resembled someone, she couldn't remember who right now. Dressed semi-casually in a white shirt with undone top buttons and blue jeans, he wasn't big and bulky, but he obviously worked out.

His skin was medium brown, the color of warm honey. He wore a faded hairstyle, tall curls on the top, shaven at the side. High cheekbones added a sculpted and refined quality to his face. A well-defined nose and neatly groomed thick eyebrows over deep-set eyes added to his appeal.

And then he smiled. His lips were dark pink, and his teeth were even white. She almost forgot to breathe.

Who was he, and why did she feel this magnetic pull?

She dragged her eyes from his and looked behind her to ensure she wasn't mistaken and that he wasn't pointing to someone behind her while she acted like a deer caught in headlights.

He raised an eyebrow when she turned around again and pointed at the chair. She walked over. He pulled out the chair for her, and she sat down, feeling a nervous jitteriness she couldn't remember feeling for any man in the past.

"Hello," he said.

"Hello," Cinnamon said, hating the breathlessness overtaking her voice.

"I was waiting for you to secure the table for us so I could get my meal and then join you."

"Er," Cinnamon swallowed, "do we know each other?"

"I doubt it. I would remember seeing you before." He smiled. "My name is Jaxon Wilde."

"Oh," Cinnamon stammered, "I've heard of you. Well, your buildings, the grand opening of your latest one was all over the news."

He smiled. "And what's your name?"

"Cinnamon Cooper," she cleared her throat.

"Cinnamon is my favorite spice," he said, "don't go anywhere; I am going to get my food, and we can chat."

She nodded obediently.

Her eyes connected with his for a moment, creating a jolt in her central nervous system. So this was what it felt like—attraction.

It had eluded her for twenty-four years of her life. And today, like a bolt out of the blue, it was here. Her nerve endings were twinging and twanging with it.

"You must tell me why you're called Cinnamon," he said after returning.

"It's a family tradition," Cinnamon said. "My great-grandmother started it, and my mother continued it. She named all three of us girls after seasonings or spices. My sister, Cayenne, is around here somewhere. And my other sister, Sage, is at university in the country."

"Cinnamon is warm, Cayenne is hot and fiery, and Sage is wise?" He raised his eyebrows. "Do the personalities match the names?"

Cinnamon chuckled. "I suppose my personality might have a hint of warmth to it. Cayenne is definitely the fiery one, always bringing that bold and passionate energy into everything she does. And Sage, let's just say she is growing in wisdom. She's still young and trying to figure it all out. I am proud of the wise choices she has made in the last couple of years."

"So, which agency are you with?" Jax asked.

"I'm sorry, I'm not a model." Cinnamon raised her long eyelashes and looked at him.

Jax inhaled ruggedly.

"It's flattering that you think I was, though."

"I came to that conclusion because you are truly beautiful," Jax murmured. "You remind me of someone."

Cinnamon's heart jolted in disappointment. He was about to say she looked like Anise. Then she would confess that Anise was her mother, and then his interest in her would either sink to the sordid where he ceased seeing her as a person and started treating her like a piece of meat, or he would judge her for having Anise as a mother.

She waited for the ax to fall, but he smiled instead.

"The fact that you are not a model is a relief. I don't date models but I would have made an exception for you. My mother was a model. And she had me at the height of her career. She dumped me on her mother and then continued working. I might have had some leftover resentment, and I'm blaming it on the profession."

Cinnamon exhaled. "Sounds likely."

Jax chuckled. "So what do you do?"

"I am an accountant," Cinnamon said.

"A noble profession," Jax nodded. "That's what I did in college, Finance and Accounting. I was planning to work in a corporate firm as a Financial Controller or something like that. Then, in my second year, I inherited a vast swath of land from my paternal grandfather. It was in a little-known area in St. Thomas; the views could rival any tourist hotspot in the world, and I said, 'Why not develop it?'"

"I spent the remainder of my college life plotting to develop it, gathered some investors, found them all on my own with a little help from my parents, and then fell in love with property development.”

Cinnamon nodded. “It sounds fun. It's like having a blank slate and doing something gorgeous with it. It's the ultimate creativity. It's on a grander scale than painting pictures.”

“That's it,” Jax smiled. “You get it. So what do you do for fun?”

“I am a homebody; I watch movies and read, and I used to do hot yoga, but I haven't gone for months now because of the sheer amount of work I have to do. I also paint pictures, but I am a rank amateur,” Cinnamon said. “I'm quite boring, actually. What do you do?”

“I play squash with my best friend Leo, I love camping in the hills, I fish, and I have a cabin in the Blue Mountains. We should go up there together sometime.”

Cinnamon gasped.

“I am sorry,” Jax smiled apologetically, a deep dimple appearing on his chin. “I am moving too fast. Do you have a boyfriend?”

“She's perennially single, never had a boyfriend, and never been kissed,” Cayenne answered behind them. “And today is her twenty-fifth birthday, a quarter century on this planet and still untouched.”

Cinnamon groaned. “I will kill you when we get home.”

“So sorry to disturb you,” Cayenne said. She smiled at Jax. “Hi, I'm Cinnamon's sister, Cayenne. I'm going to have to run down the hill for a bit. Alex locked herself out of her apartment, and I'm the one with the spare keys.”

“Oh, okay,” Cinnamon said.

“But I see you're in good hands with Jaxon Wilde; I'll be back before you know it,” Cayenne said. She turned to Jax who was staring between the two of them in fascination. “I'm your mother's hairdresser, by the way.”

“You are?” Jax smiled. “Well, you do a great job. Her hair

always looks good."

"Thank you." Cayenne smiled. "You are nice. She calls you her greatest achievement. She brags about you every chance she gets. At one point, I swear she said you walked on water."

Jax laughed. "I am pretty sure she said build on water."

"Maybe," Cayenne mused. "But because of that glowing recommendation, I trust you with my sister. I'll be back, Cinnamon. Apparently, this guy is a paragon of virtue; he feeds the poor, houses the homeless, and so on."

Cinnamon chuckled. "Well, that's good news."

"I wouldn't say paragon," Jax said when Cayenne left. "By the way, Happy Birthday. I wish I knew; I could have gotten you a present."

"Thank you, but no presents necessary; my mom says I am the one who should give presents on my birthday," Cinnamon smiled. "I can't believe you are Devina Shae's son."

"Yes, I am," Jax nodded. "I hope you won't hold it against me."

"No, I won't," Cinnamon said. "I just never put one and one together. Does that mean your father is the actor Darren Wilde? I knew you looked like someone I had seen before. I loved him in the movie Sky Dive and the River is Red."

Jax smiled. "I liked him in those movies, too."

"What's he up to these days?" Cinnamon asked. "I haven't seen him in anything lately."

"He is semi-retired from acting," Jax said. "He does mainly voice work now and has fully thrown himself into producing. He loves it."

"What do your parents do?"

Cinnamon inhaled. What should she say? That would be it if she told him she was Anise Crystal's daughter. She liked this guy. She wanted to know where this could go before she threw that particular information at him.

"My mother owns a beauty supplies shop, and I don't know who my dad is; my mother refuses to say, and I got tired of asking." She inhaled, waiting for him to act shocked that she didn't know her father and ask questions she couldn't answer.

He did something unexpected; Jax reached across the table and squeezed her fingers. It was electrifying.

She could see the response in his eyes and that he felt it too. They had insane chemistry.

He released her hands, and she reached for her water. She fumbled picking up the glass and ended up knocking it over and spilling the contents onto her clothes. The top of the glass cracked, nicking her finger.

"Your finger is bleeding," Jax said in horror. "We'll have to take a look at that."

"Oh no," Cinnamon stood up; the cold water was seeping into her dress. The glass had indeed sliced the tip of her finger. A pool of blood had gathered there and then slowly started running down her finger.

Cinnamon grabbed a napkin and covered it.

"Let's go," he said. "We can go to the pool house. There is a first aid kit in there."

Chapter Four

Cinnamon felt as if she were coming to life. Never before had she been so aware of the blood pumping through her body, of the beats of her heart, and the sensitivity of her skin. What on earth was happening to her?

Her lower body was heavy with anticipation. She felt almost intoxicated as she inhaled Jax hungrily; he was standing quite close to her. He dressed her finger, placed a bandage over it, and kissed it lightly. Her knees trembled.

She hadn't spoken to him since he led her into the spacious pool house decorated in serene blue. Watercolor paintings of sea views decorated the walls. The place had a tranquil quality to it. The music from the poolside was muted when he closed the door, but she could still hear the sounds of Marcia Griffiths and DaVille's "All My Life" playing in the background.

"Am I really here in your arms? It's just like I dreamed it would be. I feel like we're frozen in time. You're the only one I can see…"

He registered the song at the same time that she did and smiled. His smile had an inexplicable effect on her, making her feel a mix of vulnerability and exhilaration.

Their eyes met, and in that moment, she saw a depth of understanding that went beyond words. She felt as if they knew each other, like they really knew each other. Which was ridiculous; they had just met. And she was being fanciful.

Jax broke the silence with a reassuring smile, "Your finger will be just fine, Cinnamon. Do you want to get out of that dress? A robe is in the room; I'll throw it in the dryer, and it will dry in no time."

"It's just a damp area; it's not even visible," Cinnamon whispered. "There is no need for me to go through all of that."

The air between them seemed charged with an unspoken connection, a magnetic pull that neither could ignore. She cleared her throat. She needed to say something to diffuse the heavy tension.

"Er…thank you, Jax. I am not usually this clumsy. I am happy it was only water. And that the glass didn't cut me deep." Her words hung in the air, laden with a sense of gratitude and something more profound that lingered beneath the surface.

Jax's eyes held a spark of recognition as if he, too, sensed the shift in the air.

"Is it true that you have never been kissed before?" he asked softly. "Your sister was joking, right?"

Cinnamon cleared her throat. "She wasn't joking."

Jax stepped closer to her.

Cinnamon was so tense; her muscles hurt. She couldn't make herself move or drag her eyes from him.

She knew what Jax was going to do. They were going to kiss. Her first kiss. Her heart was beating so hard she felt it in her ears. The anticipation hung thick in the air, creating a charged atmosphere that seemed to envelop them both.

Jax's eyes held a mixture of warmth and understanding as if he could sense the excitement and nervousness coursing through her veins.

He lifted a strand of her hair away from her face. The simple gesture sent shivers down her spine, and she found herself leaning into his touch almost involuntarily. Time seemed to slow as he cupped her cheek, his thumb grazing lightly over her lower lip.

Cinnamon's breath caught in her throat as Jax leaned in, closing the distance between them. The world outside the pool house ceased to exist, leaving only the hushed sounds of their shared breaths and the rhythmic thud of their hearts in the quiet space.

His breath fanned her cheek. He let his tongue dart between her parted lips, and she jerked and moaned and reached up for him.

He did it again, and her whole body leaped, electrified. Just one kiss, she promised herself. This did not make her wanton or like her mother in any way. This was something most women had experienced way before her.

He pressed his mouth to her cheek, brow, and lowered eyelids, teasing her with feather-light kisses until she strained up to him even more.

And then he kissed her lips. She melted to boiling point in seconds. He made love to her mouth with an intimacy that shook her.

And then he stopped.

"We have to stop now," he said roughly. "Join the outside world, or this can get very intimate quickly. My control is slipping."

Cinnamon nodded dazedly. What about her control? She had well and truly lost it.

They went out and joined the party. Many people were out on the dance floor. Somebody had cleared their table, and other people were sitting there.

Dennis Brown's "How Could I Leave" was playing.

"Would you like to dance with me, madam?" Jax asked her.

Cinnamon blinked, still feeling the remnants of the moment they shared in the pool house. She managed a small smile and nodded in response to Jax's invitation.

"I'd love to," she said, her voice carrying a mix of excitement and lingering shyness. "I love old-school reggae."

Jax took her hand, leading her to the dance floor where the rhythmic beats of the music echoed. The dance floor became their own private world, a space where the outside pressures faded away, leaving only the connection between them.

They moved in harmony, caught up in the music and the subtle intimacy between them.

"Promise you won't leave me, promise you won't hurt me," Dennis Brown's melodious voice floated over them. Both Cinnamon and Jax sang along to the song.

The night unfolded with laughter, shared stories, and more dances. They navigated the party together as if they were glued at the side.

It was almost irritating to Cinnamon when Cayenne found her and whispered, "I know you are having fun, but it's ten o'clock. You said this was your cut-off time."

"Oh," Cinnamon inhaled ruggedly. "It is. My day is crazy tomorrow."

"I knew you'd have fun." Cayenne chuckled.

"I should get going," she said to Jax.

Jax tightened his hand around hers. "Give me your number."

He fished his phone out of his pocket and handed it to her.

"I'll call you before you reach home, and you'll have mine." He said when she handed him the phone.

Cinnamon punched in her number in his phone and handed it back. "It was nice to meet you."

He kissed her hard, in full view of everyone around. "Likewise."

Chapter Five

"I can't believe I had such a good time," Cinnamon said with a satisfied smile. "It was the best birthday ever, filled with firsts. If I knew kisses were that erotic, and I could feel that way, I would have kissed someone a long time ago."

"It's not like that with everyone; you lucked out," Cayenne looked at her and grinned. "My first kiss with Gavin Peterson was a horrendous mess. Uh."

Cinnamon sank further into the passenger side of the car, a pleased smile on her face.

"So what now?" Cayenne asked. "Are you going to be dating the rich, handsome Jaxon Wilde? A man with his name on several buildings all over the country?"

"I wouldn't mind it," Cinnamon said.

"Cinnamon Jade Wilde has a ring to it," Cayenne chuckled.

Cinnamon sat up straighter, "Oh my God, I forgot."

"What?" Cayenne asked.

"That my mother is Anise Crystal," she groaned.

"So?" Cayenne asked.

"So a man like Jax will not date someone like me, even though we strike sparks off each other. He'll find out about me sooner or later and drop me like a hot potato."

"Well," Cayenne nodded, "you might have a point; his mother is now dating Nelson Greystone."

"And you didn't think to tell me that! They are taking Anise to court," Cinnamon groaned. "Why did we even go to the party in the first place?"

"So that you could have a good time, be kissed for the first time, and meet a guy who turned your world upside down. It's about time."

"But Cayenne," Cinnamon fretted, "this is madness, you know that, right? Does Devina know you are Anise's daughter?"

"Hell no," Cayenne said. "I tend not to tell people that little fact."

"You can get away with it because you don't look like her," Cinnamon muttered. "Lucky you."

"I look like my father, the pedophile, unlucky me," Cayenne said.

"I don't know who my father is," Cinnamon rejoined, "and he probably was a pedophile too; my mother had me at thirteen. So double unlucky me."

They glanced at each other and grinned. Nobody won when they decided to compare their lot in life.

"Wasn't this birthday supposed to be the big reveal?" Cayenne asked. "Wasn't this the year Mom said she would spill it all?"

"She's been saying that since I was eighteen, and then twenty-one, and then every year after that. 'It's next year, Cinna, don't be impatient. The story around your conception is horrible.'

"I have since stopped asking because I don't want to hear why it was horrible."

"What if you are related to Jax?" Cayenne asked. "You would have just kissed your brother."

"Ew," Cinnamon mused, "you have a point. I deserve to know."

"That's right," Cayenne said. "She doesn't have to give details, just the bare facts and a name. She doesn't even have to tell you; she could text it to you."

"Hmmph," Cinnamon said. "She texted me happy birthday. I'll just ask her to text a name."

They drove up to their townhouse, and Anise Crystal was there, just getting out of her car with a big gift basket in hand. She was dressed like she was going to a party. She was in a green wig, matching green lipstick, and accessories.

"Speaking of the devil," Cinnamon murmured, "she did buy me a gift this year. Last year, she tried to avoid me like I had the plague. She does seem to fall apart around my birthday like clockwork."

"My babies," Anise said, "I have a thing tonight, and I didn't want to forget your birthday this year, Cinna. Happy birthday, my dearest one. I am happy you went out. Did you have a good time?" She air-kissed Cinnamon and handed her the gift basket.

"Yes, I did. It was great. And thank you for the gift."

"Lovely to hear, dear. Toodles."

"Wait a minute, mom," Cinnamon said. "Aren't you forgetting something? You promised to tell me who is my father. You said you'd tell me on my birthday this year."

"Oh, Cinnamon. Why do you need a father? Fathers are severely overrated; trust me on that."

"Can I at least get a name?" Cinnamon asked, hating the plea that was in her voice. Did it matter that much to her?

After all these years? Yes, it did. Everybody deserved to know who their father was.

Anise sighed. She dangled her car keys in her long-manicured fingers and looked between her and Cayenne. Anise cleared her throat and then looked off into the distance. "I guess I owe you the truth, don't I? You have been such a good girl. You aren't addicted to drugs or fallen into bad company, and I am not a grandmother. I expected to be a grandmother by now. My grandma had my mom at twenty, my mom had me when she was twenty, I had you at thirteen… it's nice to know you are bucking the trend."

"We all bucked the trend," Cayenne said, "well, Sage is nineteen; the jury is still out on that one."

"And I am proud of all my girls," Anise said, dramatically batting her long green eyelashes.

Cinnamon rolled her eyes. "Can we stay on topic here?"

"The point I was making is, I am super proud of you, Cinna," Anise said, "you finished college, you are holding down a job, and you live a decent life."

"Thanks, mom," Cinnamon said. "But…"

"She kissed a guy tonight," Cayenne interjected, "he could be her brother. Can you imagine if he was?"

"Oh my," Anise said, "who was it?"

"Jax Wilde," Cayenne said eagerly.

"Nope, not your brother. You are not related, not in the least. I never even met his father. He is handsome, though." Anise mused. "Good for you, Cinna. Jax Wilde is a fabulous catch. The only strike against him is that he is close to Noreen Greystone and the whole family. He will not be pleased to hear you are related to me."

"I kind of figured that out myself," Cinnamon sighed.

"I don't know how you will be able to hide your relation to me, though," Anise said ruefully, "Noreen is going to take me to court; only her precious family should inherit Greystone shares."

"Why did Richard Greystone leave you his money and shares in his company?" Cinnamon asked.

"Because he is a generous, kind man who loves to share with the less fortunate," Anise grinned.

"So you can't tell us?" Cinnamon asked, "We have to find out stuff from the news? Like we do for every aspect of your life?"

"Don't listen to the news, sweetie," Anise said, "they are usually wrong."

"Was he your lover?" Cayenne asked.

Anise laughed. "That's gross. Contrary to popular opinion, I am not a prostitute. I was one for a very brief point in my life, and that was by necessity. I have dated and broken up with men who admittedly are newsworthy, but that's all in the past. I am now celibate."

Cayenne widened her eyes, "you are?"

"Yes, seven days and counting."

Cinnamon and Cayenne laughed.

"That's not long," Cinnamon said, "are you sure you aren't a sex addict?"

"I might be," Anise shrugged, "we'll find out after this experiment. I have to go; my party beckons." Anise got into her car.

"Wait, Mom," Cinnamon said urgently, "all I want is a name."

Anise wound down her car window. "I've been keeping the secret for twenty-five years. Do you expect I would just blurt out a name without any context in the parking lot of a townhouse complex where anyone can listen in? Besides, I need alcohol or some relaxant before I'll be ready to tell you. Yes, I'll need to be medicated to dredge up all of that mess from twenty-five years ago."

Cinnamon groaned.

"You know what?" After starting the car, Anise said, "If your grandmother is willing to tell you, then I will. But I promised to keep my mouth shut and I have."

"What does Nana have to do with this?" Cinnamon asked, confused. "I thought you had run away from home…"

"Oh girl, your Nana knows everything," Anise said. "I was going to tell you the whole story when you were eighteen, and she shut me up by giving you this house in exchange for my silence. When I was ready to tell you at twenty-one, she bought you a car. Your sneaky Nana has been buying my silence for years now by paying for your college and buying you stuff. When I finally get my money from the Greystones, I'll be the wealthy one and I will sing like a canary, but until then, I promised your Nana my silence. I always keep my promises even if they are distasteful."

Anise tooted them and drove off.

"I always wondered why Nana got me this house and a car," Cinnamon muttered. "Now I find out it's a hush money payment."

"It really is a huge secret," Cayenne said.

"It does seem so," Cinnamon grunted. "But all of this secrecy makes me wonder who my father is."

Cayenne nodded. "It's intriguing."

"Who do you think my father is?" Cinnamon asked Cayenne as she opened the front door.

Their townhouse was the typical layout for their neighborhood. A tiny kitchenette to the left, a small dining area, then a living room area. Upstairs had three bedrooms and two bathrooms.

"Let's recap what we know of our dear mother's life, shall we?" Cayenne said.

"Let's do that," Cinnamon placed the heavy gift basket on the dining table.

"So she ran away from home at twelve," Cayenne said, "and went to live with friends for a few weeks."

Cinnamon nodded.

"When they found her, she ran away again and went missing for months. And they never knew where she was."

"Grandma said she lived in a house with other girls, and when they found her, she was six months pregnant with me," Cinnamon sighed. "I assumed no one knew who impregnated her."

"I think it's the senator," Cayenne said. "Why else would he leave her money and shares?"

"He was eighty years old when he died," Cinnamon said. "Mom is thirty-eight now. That would have been an age gap of forty-two years. He would have been in his sixties while messing around with a thirteen-year-old. That's sick."

"Yep," Cayenne nodded. "That's your dad."

"Stop it!" Cinnamon chuckled. "Maybe I shouldn't push Mom to tell me anything. In the future, if I am dating anyone, I'll ask her if the guy and I are related."

"And what if she is not around?" Cayenne wiggled her eyebrows. "What if she loses her memory or her mind? How will you know?"

"You have a point," Cinnamon admitted.

"Besides, I think Jax is your person. I can feel it."

"Jax might not want to talk to me when he learns who's my mom," Cinnamon said. "I am gearing up for it."

"Which would be too bad," Cayenne sighed. "Let me see what she got you."

Cayenne opened the cavernous basket. "Ooh, snacks, underwear, and flavored condoms."

Cinnamon groaned. "By the time I get around to using the

condoms, they'll be flavorless."

Cayenne giggled. "You'll use them; you're now a woman of the world."

"One kiss does not make me a woman of the world," Cinnamon snorted. "Besides, he may not keep in touch."

Her phone pinged with a message almost at the same time.

"Hi Cinnamon, It's Jax. Save this number. I am already missing you. What are your plans for the weekend?"

"At least he doesn't know who I am yet," Cinnamon whispered.

"He may not care," Cayenne said. "Go with the flow. Tell him the truth; you have no plans for this weekend or any weekend for that matter, your life is as dry and flaky as three-month unwashed hair."

Cinnamon glared at her sister.

Cayenne cackled in laughter.

Chapter Six

The day after the party Jax drove into Moretti Bedding and parked. It was way after ten, a later-than-usual start for him, but he had promised his brother he would pay him a visit, and he was true to his word.

It had taken him a little while to fall asleep after the party last night. He had relived the kiss with Cinnamon over and over again. It hadn't made for a peaceful night's sleep. He had ended up sleeping in the pool house instead of going downhill, and it was as if her perfume had lingered in the room.

What was it about this particular woman that had him in such a chokehold? He felt an urgency to see her again, hear her voice, kiss her again, every day until eternity. He was feeling that sappy.

He needed to get a hold of himself; he had business to take care of. His brother needed his help. He had to be sharp and switch to business mode.

The office parking lot was looking a little worse for wear. There were trucks parked at the side with the Moretti Bedding logo on the side and rusted bed springs in a pile in the corner. The office building needed a lick of paint, and the warehouse area had all sorts of debris at the front. It wasn't the most enticing entrance. He would be depressed showing up for work at what looked like a junkyard. He couldn't recall it being this bad when Lorenzo had run the place. Marco needed to do better.

He parked under a fully loaded mango tree, walked up a flight of stairs, and entered the receptionist area. Luckily, the inside looked much better than the outside. The receptionist was playing a game on the computer. She looked up when he entered and smiled at him widely.

"Oh my, you're handsome."

It was a very unprofessional greeting. Jax glowered at her.

"Is Mr. Moretti in?"

"He is," her smile dimmed somewhat. "Who should I say is here to see him?"

"Jax Wilde," he said impatiently.

"Oh, Mr. Wilde," her eyes widened. "He's been expecting you; his office is the last door at the end."

"Thank you," Jax nodded briskly.

The walk down was just a long line of cubicles with the managers of the various departments in glass-enclosed offices. He passed HR, Marketing and Sales, and Accounts. He paused at Accounts. Marco was bending over, looking at the screen of his account manager, his hand lightly touching her shoulder in what he could only describe as a caress. He would recognize that neck anywhere, the curve of her cheek, the smoothness of her skin. It was Cinnamon.

Marco's account manager was Cinnamon!

He was confused for a second. Cinnamon had not said

where she worked in all their talks last night. And he hadn't thought to ask. Jealousy hit him like a freight train. They were intently looking at the screen together, their heads unnecessarily close.

"You are here to see Marco," an older lady in a black pants suit stood beside him.

"Yes," Jax murmured, "but I see he is otherwise occupied. Are you waiting for him, too?"

"Yes," the lady snorted. "My name is on the door, but as you can see, they have kicked me out of what used to be my office and are having secret meetings without me. I used to believe hard work and mastering your craft was enough to push you forward, but I guess being pretty and having the boss hanging onto your every word is the way to move forward these days."

"Is that so?" Jax stiffened. He looked at the door, and it said Sheila Mendez, Account Manager.

"Yes, it's so," Sheila snorted. "Maybe if I looked like a perfect Barbie doll and had a killer shape, I wouldn't be demoted." She walked off in a huff.

Jax knocked briefly on the glass. Both Marco and Cinnamon looked up. Marco had a huge smile on his face, and Cinnamon looked shocked. He glared at her for a full minute. Last night, she had struck him as different. He had really bought the story that it had been her first kiss. She had kissed him back so innocently. He had liked the fantasy of being there for all her firsts.

She probably had a good laugh at his expense when she had gone home with her sister. It didn't escape him that she was looking good even now under the harsh fluorescent light. She had the kind of face that would look good in any light.

Was that guilt in her eyes? Did she know that Marco was

his brother? Was Cinnamon the girl at the office that Marco was insinuating he wanted to cheat on Ella with? Was that why he had demoted the bitter lady he had just spoken to?

He dragged his gaze from her and focused on Marco, giving him a fulsome glare. Marco quickly wiped the smile off his face while Cinnamon shifted uncomfortably in her chair.

"In your office, please," he said.

Marco nodded. "Sure."

"I just spoke with Sheila. She seems to believe her demotion is linked to factors other than her performance. Care to enlighten me?" Jax asked as soon as Marco closed the door to his office, which was chaotic and untidy. Jax wondered how he got any work done.

"Sheila's work hasn't been up to par lately, and we had to make some adjustments for the sake of the team," Marco cleared his throat.

Jax arched an eyebrow, unconvinced. "Are you sure about that? Sheila mentioned secret meetings and feeling excluded. If I am going to invest in this company, I need transparency and won't tolerate any unfair practices."

Marco hurriedly moved a stack of boxes from his chair and asked Jax to sit. "We installed a new accounting software; we were just trying to streamline processes between purchasing accounts and the warehouse. Sheila is not tech-savvy, and she didn't take it well. She doesn't want to attend training; she thinks it's beneath her.

"I inherited her from Dad and didn't want to fire her like that. To tell you the truth, I need more people in accounts, and even though Sheila is a tough old bird, I need her right now. So I had to demote her. Payroll is in two days. I am overworking poor Cinnamon; I don't know if she'll stay with us under these conditions."

"Oh," Jax exhaled. "Sheila implied you were having an affair."

"Goodness no. Cinnamon is gorgeous, but she's one of Ella's closest girlfriends. If I made a pass at her, she would tell Ella. And then I would be dead."

Jax chuckled. Ella had Marco living in fear of the consequences of him cheating. Good.

"Besides that, Cinnamon is not that into men." Marco continued. "Ella says she has never had a boyfriend. I think she is in the closet."

Jax smiled. Now, that was not true. He knew that she was into men. She was into him. Her response to him last night was well and truly genuine. The thought made him feel good.

He sat down at the desk and changed the topic. "The first order of business is to get a team of cleaners here and outside. Then I will get two of my accountants in here to assist Cinnamon, and then I will have to meet with Sheila."

"Yes!" Marco nodded.

****

It was the end of the day. There was a slight pounding going on behind her eyes. The office had been very busy, almost electrified. She had found out along the way, by Marco, that Jax Wilde was a potential investor, and he was looking at the books. She was supposed to cooperate fully. A steady stream of new faces had walked in and out of her office, asking her for clarification on certain accounting matters. She was completely fried between that and the new accounting software, giving her problems with payroll because Sheila had uploaded the wrong data.

She vaguely recalled Sheila coming to the door at

lunchtime.

"I am sorry," Sheila said dourly.

"For what?" Cinnamon had asked, startled.

"For implying that you were having an affair with Marco, and that's why I was demoted."

"Okay," Cinnamon nodded. "Who did you imply this to?"

"His brother Jaxon Wilde. He is sending me off to training at his office uptown. I will be fired if I don't learn the new software."

"Oh," Cinnamon was confused. "I guess he will be in charge for the next couple of months," Sheila said. "Expect some changes around here."

Jax Wilde was Marco Moretti's brother? They looked nothing alike. Jax was tall, dark, and handsome, and Marco was short, light, and average.

Besides, Marco never mentioned he was related to his more famous relatives. Not once.

She stared at Sheila's retreating back.

Jax was going to be her boss for the next few months? She figured that he had worked out who she was and she was expecting to be fired.

She hadn't seen him since he had disappeared in the direction of Marco's office. And as the day went on and she got more immersed in work, she realized that she wouldn't know if he had passed her office. She had been that focused. She hadn't even spent much time speculating about her impending firing.

"Cinnamon," he appeared at her office door as if she had conjured him up.

She swallowed. This was it; he would accuse her of being deceitful by not telling him who she really was and having some affair with his brother. Then, he would ask her to leave.

She glanced at the clock. It was six thirty-five.

He looked at it, too. "I have an apology to make. Can we go out to dinner?"

"You mean you are not going to fire me?" Cinnamon raised a weary brow.

"No, I planned to do the opposite—grovel at your feet. You are quite a good accountant. My financial advisor was impressed; Marco can't afford to lose someone with your skills."

Cinnamon exhaled. She had braced herself for the worst, but his unexpected response left her momentarily speechless.

"I don't understand why you were so mad this morning," she stammered, her brow still furrowed. "Was it about what Sheila said? She came to apologize."

He sighed and entered the office, closing the door behind him. "I've been a fool. I jumped to conclusions and made assumptions about you and Marco. I didn't know you worked here. My assumptions were not without merit; he mentioned being interested in someone here, and I assumed it was you. I mean, who else could it be? You are the most beautiful woman in the world. And since last night, I have been thinking about you on a loop."

Cinnamon smiled; he called her the most beautiful woman in the world.

"So, I am not going to be fired then?" she asked cautiously.

He chuckled, "Absolutely not. In fact, I'm hoping you'll accept my apology and join me for dinner. I'd like to make it up to you and prove that I'm not the paranoid guy you must have thought I was."

Cinnamon smiled. "Dinner sounds good."

"And I promise never to jump to conclusions about you again," Jax said.

Cinnamon frowned. "You promise?"

"Promise," Jax said. "I'll give you the benefit of the doubt from here on out."

Chapter Seven

That may have been a promise he won't be able to keep, Cinnamon thought fatalistically. That would be out the window as soon as he finds out who her mother was.

They went to the Wilde Building for dinner. It was Cinnamon's first time in a building like it, a residential luxury building with all the amenities. She had been in awe from the moment they entered the private parking lot.

"I see why all the newspapers were gushing over this," she whispered. "It's awesome. And I haven't been inside yet."

Jax chuckled, "We were going for understated luxury and elegance to create a space that residents won't want to leave if you don't want to. Our amenities include a state-of-the-art fitness center, a rooftop infinity pool with breathtaking views of the city skyline, and a private spa that offers personalized treatments. We also have a gourmet restaurant on the ground floor, a cozy lounge for residents to socialize, and a truly spectacular restaurant on the top floor overlooking the city and the mountains in the distance."

When they entered the lobby, Cinnamon kept whispering, "Oh my gosh. It's nice."

Jax chuckled. "Your response is actually what we were going for. All the floors were sold out on showing the virtual building alone."

The concierge greeted them warmly, "Good evening, Mr. Wilde. How are you?"

"Great, Miles," Jax responded. "This is Miss Cooper. I hope she will be making many visits here."

Cinnamon smiled at Miles and then looked at Jax. "Do you live here too?"

"Yes," Jax nodded. "There are six penthouse apartments; I kept one. This is the most complex building I have ever done; it's my greatest accomplishment so far. I had to live here for the experience. I can give you a tour after we eat."

They made their way to the elevator that would take them to the restaurant on the top floor. Once they reached the rooftop, Cinnamon was mesmerized by the panoramic view of the city. The evening lights shimmered below. The restaurant was aptly named the Orchids. It had large Orchid centerpieces at each table and had hanging baskets around the room.

The décor was chic, the lighting dim, and the music soft and melodic, creating a sophisticated and relaxing ambiance.

The waiter led them to a table by the edge, offering an unobstructed view of the city lights and the distant mountains.

"This is beyond anything I could have imagined. It's like a dream up here," Cinnamon remarked.

Jax grinned. "I'm glad you think so. So where were we? I need to apologize for being an ass today. I almost let my brother have it when I saw his hand on your shoulder."

Cinnamon smiled. "I had no idea that you were related to Marco, that his mother was Devina Shae, his brother was Jax Wilde or anything. He and Ella live in a cramped apartment in Halfway Tree, and he drives a car on its last legs. He is so stingy with money; we almost come to blows on the yearly budget."

Jax laughed.

"Does Ella know about you guys?"

"Yes, she does," Jax nodded. "We consider Ella to be family now. Marco doesn't mention us because he is determined to do things on his own without our interference. His father left him the company when he returned to Italy a few years ago. He was going to sell it, but Marco said he would run it. Lorenzo was skeptical, we were all skeptical. I think that gave Marco a chip on his shoulder.

He wants to show us all that he can succeed with it. He only asked for my help recently because he knows the company needs to grow or die."

Cinnamon nodded. "I gave him that speech."

Jax smiled. "Well, thank you for talking some sense into him."

"So, can we play twenty questions?" Jax asked, "So that I can get to know you better and not jump to conclusions again?"

"Sure," Cinnamon smiled.

"How do you look so good at a party, at work and after work?"

Cinnamon laughed. "Genetics and clean living."

"Why is it that you don't have a boyfriend? I can't imagine why men aren't clamoring to knock down your door."

"Mmm, let me see," Cinnamon mused, "I suppose it's a combination of factors. I've focused more on my career and personal growth over the last couple of years and haven't actively sought a relationship. Plus, I believe in letting things happen organically. I want a connection that goes beyond appearances and fits seamlessly into my life."

Jax nodded. "That makes sense. Quality over quantity, right?"

Cinnamon smiled. "Exactly. I'd rather wait for the right person than rush into something that doesn't feel authentic. I have seen my mother kiss a lot of frogs, hunting for her prince. I don't want that for myself. It looks exhausting."

"Yes, it does," Jax nodded. "That's exactly why I am a take it slow kind of guy."

Cinnamon smiled.

Jax continued with the questions, his curiosity sparking a lively conversation. They delved into topics ranging from favorite books and travel destinations to childhood memories and dreams for the future.

They paused long enough to order; Cinnamon chose the roast chicken, and Jax chose a vegetarian option.

"Not vegetarian," he said when she asked, "but I love the Chana Masala here. Next time you come back, you have to try it."

"Okay," Cinnamon said happily; he expected her to return. She would happily do so.

As the evening progressed and they ordered their food, Cinnamon opened up more than expected.

Jax, too, shared anecdotes and insights about himself.

She was shocked to discover he was a lead singer in his school choir.

"You were?" Cinnamon raised her eyebrows.

"And here's another thing that many people don't know about me," Jax said, "I will hog a karaoke machine at a party all night if they let me."

Cinnamon laughed.

"And despite my high-octane work, I find solace in simple pleasures. I sometimes escape to my cabin in the mountains to recharge; that's where I am most comfortable and creative. I love hiking, fishing, and being alone with my thoughts."

Cinnamon's eyes lit up with intrigue. "I would have never guessed that about you."

The revelation added a new layer to Jax's persona, and Cinnamon appreciated the complexity beneath his polished exterior. She was about to say more when she heard her grandmother's voice.

Rosemary Landry's voice was distinctive. She had worked in radio for over thirty years for one of those current affairs programs, and she taught Media Communications at the university for almost as long. She was talking to someone at the door, accompanied by her husband, Dr. Timothy Landry, or Grandpop.

Grandpop was a teddy bear of a man, lovable and sweet; he was warmth personified, making up for the coldness of Rosemary. It was not common knowledge that Rosemary was Anise Crystal's mother; Anise and Rosemary had long parted ways and didn't have much of a relationship. Even though her grandmother lived in the same town and neighborhood as she did, she wasn't close to her either. Rosemary was not close to any of the grandchildren her only child had given her. Cinnamon didn't know if that was good or bad; she was neutral on the issue.

Her grandmother was certainly nobody's idea of a warm, fuzzy little old lady who baked cookies and fussed over her. She was a fifty-eight-year-old woman who could pass for a couple of years younger, having cut off all her hair and sported a low cut. She dyed her graying hair a vibrant red, worked out quite consistently, and it showed. She was tall and gorgeous and was the type of person to kiss you twice on each cheek and call you "darling." Cinnamon had always found her both intimidating and intriguing at the same time.

She was sometimes sad that she preferred Grandpop over Nana. Nana was her biological relative. Grandpop spotted her first. He came over and greeted her, kissing her on the forehead.

"Hello, my precious."

"Hello, Grandpop," Cinnamon smiled. "Meet Jaxon Wilde, my date."

"Hello, Jax," Grandpop smiled at Jax. "I have not seen you in years. I think that is a good thing."

Jax laughed. "It definitely is."

They knew each other, obviously.

"Honey, meet Jax," he turned to his wife, "he is on a date with our Cinnamon."

"Interesting," Rosemary smiled. "Lovely to meet you, Jax. This is a fabulous building. Our only regret is that we didn't buy in when the apartments were first put on the market; they went so fast."

Jax smiled.

"Darling," her grandmother kissed her on the cheek.

"Nana," Cinnamon said weakly.

"Let us leave the young people, Tim."

They left them to be seated. Cinnamon looked at Jax. "That's my granny and her husband."

Jax laughed. "It's a small world. Dr. Tim was my childhood doctor, and I didn't know that your grandmother is the formidable Rosemary Landry. When she hosts a party, you know it's sophisticated."

"That's right," Cinnamon nodded. "That's my Nana Rosie."

****

"What are you doing this weekend?" Jax walked her to the parking lot after dinner. She had declined a tour of his penthouse. She was feeling bone tired.

"I am planning to get some sleep," she stifled a yawn, "and maybe visit Grandma Sadie on Sunday. What are you doing?"

"I might go up to my cabin in the hills. Come with me."

"I ah," Cinnamon opened her mouth. "I…"

"The cabin has four bedrooms," Jax hurriedly added. "I am severely attracted to you, but it's just an invitation, no pressure. It's not a thinly veiled invite to have sex. We can come back in time for your visit to your grandma."

Cinnamon hesitated momentarily; her tiredness forgotten as she looked into Jax's eyes. His expression showed sincerity and kindness, and she found herself warming up to the idea.

"It's been a while since I've had a break, and spending some time in the hills sounds tempting. I am a city girl through and through, so don't judge me if I act like it."

Jax grinned, "Great! We can unwind, enjoy the scenery, and maybe even hike if you're up for it. Plus, my cabin is pretty secluded, so it's a perfect escape from the daily grind, and the sleep is always better up there. It's getting cold now; I'll text you a list of things to take."

Cinnamon nodded, "Okay, it sounds lovely," she admitted.

Jax walked her to her car and kissed her briefly on the lips. "Goodnight, see you tomorrow."

Chapter Eight

"I can't believe you are going away for the weekend with Jaxon Wilde," Cayenne said, watching from the doorway as she packed her bag on Thursday night. "You just met him two days ago, and since then, you kissed him, and now you are going away with him for the weekend. Who are you, and what have you done with my sensible sister?"

"I am still sensible," Cinnamon laughed. "He is not an ax murderer; he is Jaxon Wilde. Nana called me and said she was impressed that I found such an upstanding man to keep company with."

"Don't forget these," Cayenne handed her a pack of condoms that were in the gift basket. "You are moving like the Flash since meeting this guy; you may need them."

Cinnamon looked at the condoms wide-eyed. "What do people do with flavored condoms?"

"What do I know?" Cayenne shrugged. "Ask your mother. She is the one that gave them to you."

Cinnamon laughed. "She has a way of being too graphic in her explanations; I'll search for the info on the Internet. It will be way milder than Anise."

Cayenne nodded, "Good idea."

"I won't need them, though," Cinnamon said, taking them and placing them in her bag. "And I definitely won't let Jax know I have them. It would send the wrong message."

Cayenne nodded. "I don't need to tell you to slow down and develop feelings first, do I?"

"You don't need to tell me," Cinnamon said. "I think I gave you the same speech a couple of years ago when you had that hopeless crush on that guy next door, who you were determined to sleep with. What was his name again?"

"You know perfectly well his name was Lance Cauldwell, studious, nerdy, loveable Lance," Cayenne cleared her throat. "He migrated before we could do anything. I'll always regret that."

Cinnamon raised an eyebrow. "I don't think he migrated; I think he escaped you."

"It still hurts that he left," Cayenne frowned, "It still sticks in my craw that he didn't have the decency to tell me goodbye. One minute, he was there, and then poof, next, he was gone. Not even a note, and no forwarding address. I loved him to the depths of my young heart. What if I ever get into a serious relationship, and the guy proposes? In that case, I will go and seek out Lance Cauldwell and make sure I feel nothing before I proceed. What I felt for him wasn't normal. It was heavy like our souls knew each other."

Cinnamon stopped packing and laughed, tumbling in the bed with uncontrolled mirth.

"What is it about the nerd boys that I find so attractive?" Cayenne mused, "I really am drawn to that type. The more bookish and uptight they are, the more I want to break down their barriers. But we are not talking about me. We are talking about you. Take time to know him; it's not just an overnight thing."

Cinnamon laughed. "Really, you are quoting Percy Sledge to me? I have taken nothing but time. I am a twenty-five-year-old virgin. I am this way because I am mindful of all the speeches and the pitfalls. I have gotten this far; I will be fine, thank you very much."

****

Jax picked her up at home a little after six. The traffic had eased up somewhat. When they left the city behind, Cinnamon was feeling a little lighter and free. It was funny how that worked. It's as if the city was suffocating and had pinned her down.

"Tough week?" Jax looked over at her and smiled.

"Yep," Cinnamon nodded. "My interim boss, Mr. Jax Wilde, came and took over the company where I work and gave me some additional tasks to do on top of what I had."

Jax smiled, "But Mr. Wilde also gave you two competent accountants to work with, expanded your department overnight, and now you have a streamlined system."

Cinnamon nodded. "I am grateful for that. When Sheila returns, I don't know where she will fit in. She hates technology."

"She sent in her resignation this evening," Jax said, "the training was not working out."

"She needs to deal with her technology phobia," Cinnamon said. "She won't get a job in our field if she doesn't. She was a good accountant, though. I kind of felt bad when I was promoted over her."

"Don't ever feel bad about being promoted; you earned

it. Sheila's resignation is unfortunate, but adapting to technological advancements is crucial in today's professional landscape. Marco needs to modernize and improve the efficiency of the company. Everyone in the team must embrace these changes to stay competitive."

Cinnamon nodded and inhaled. "I fully agree. I am looking forward to the challenge and adventure this weekend. I can honestly say I have never been past Papine.

"I look forward to seeing what the view is like in the morning. What possessed you to buy a cabin in the hills?"

"I got it at a good price from Richard Greystone," Jax said. "It felt more like a gift. In recent years, I was the only one who would make the trek up here with him."

Cinnamon turned to him, "Senator Greystone?"

"Yup," Jax nodded. "He was a close family friend. You know, friends that are like family. That's what the Greystones are to my family.

"We used to come up here with him, fish, hike, and camp. He would tell me stories of the good old days. I was the only one who was as into it as he was. His sons, grandchildren, or wife weren't as keen to join us, and if they did, lots of complaining went on. There was no internet or cell phone signal. It didn't matter that we told the complainers that that was the point of coming up here to cut out the distractions and really get to know each other."

Cinnamon nodded. "So that's why you invited me up here. You want to get to know me."

"Yes," Jax flashed a smile at her. "I like you. I am not prevaricating on that. I really, really like you. I think the cabin can fast-track our getting to know each other. I'll see what you look like without a pound of makeup and hear your opinion on many topics."

"I am not wearing any makeup now. I haven't worn any all

week," Cinnamon sputtered, "a pound of makeup, really?"

Jax laughed. "I know you are naturally beautiful, Cinnamon. I was just teasing."

"Tell me about Richard Greystone," Cinnamon said, her curiosity about the man who had left her mother a fortune was at a fever pitch.

"You are curious because you heard about the lawsuit contesting the will?" Jax sighed. "The whole thing was shocking to me."

"Why?" Cinnamon asked.

"The Richard that I know was a man of integrity. A true gentleman. I can't imagine him cheating on Noreen with a woman fifty years his junior. He is the one who has always told me that if you want to cheat, let your partner know and be prepared to let her go. I dated his granddaughter, Carissa, for five years. That was our motto because of Richard, and we took it seriously. She wanted to cheat, so we broke up."

"Oh, I didn't know that," Cinnamon said.

"Yes," Jax sighed. "We were engaged and lived together for two years. Early last year, Richard took me aside at the New Year's Eve party that Greystone Wines throws annually. He said, 'You do not want to marry Carissa, or you would have by now. Do not settle with her. You'll be a thousand times happier, and she will be too. You are not supposed to work so hard at loving someone that it's exhausting. It's supposed to flow naturally. You are supposed to want to be around them all the time, miss them when they leave, and every day thank God that you found them.'"

"Oh wow," Cinnamon said.

"I assumed he was talking about him and Noreen; they've been married for so long and have a good partnership going," Jax said. "Now, I am not so sure he was talking about his wife of over fifty years since Anise Crystal is on the scene."

Cinnamon cleared her throat. "What do you think about her?"

"What is there to think?" Jax shrugged. "She didn't force Richard to leave her his money and shares in his company. I know that Richard was not a man who was easily persuaded to do anything he didn't want to do. He must have had her in high regard. I don't know why that may be, but he did. He had to."

Cinnamon cleared her throat. "That's the fairest assessment I've heard about the situation. Usually, people bring up her past, think she is a gold digger, paint her as some femme fatale who divided a family."

"I knew Richard Greystone," Jax said, "I was probably closer to him than his own sons and grandsons. We spent quite a lot of time up here in these hills, just talking and ruminating about life. He wasn't some weak old man who could be easily snared by a woman. I know this much, whatever Anise Crystal was to him, he had some emotions invested in her."

"As for the innuendos about her past as a prostitute," Jax snorted, "I don't know if people realize they are describing a child who ran away from home and was selling herself as a prostitute; that should not be sensationalized in the least. All of the adults in her life should have been locked up for whatever drove a child to that state.

"And it doesn't take a genius to see that her early life contributed to her cycling through partners. She was probably searching for that love she never got as a child. Maybe she got that acceptance with Richard; not every relationship had to be sexual. Maybe she saw a father figure in him. Who knows?"

Cinnamon smiled in the dark. This was the pivotal moment that she knew that she definitely and positively loved Jaxon

Wilde. This response summed him up as a human being. He was a fair and balanced individual.

She cleared her throat. "What was the Greystone family like?"

"Tight knit. There are three sons, Nelson, Nicholas, and Nolan. Ten grandchildren and around three great-grandchildren so far. They run several businesses under the Greystone group of companies, so they have to work together."

"His sons' names all begin with N," Cinnamon chuckled.

"Well, his wife's name is Noreen," Jax mused. "It makes sense."

"Were they in love?" Cinnamon asked.

"I thought so. They have been together forever," Jax said. "They were good friends and partners. Their offices were side by side. I don't think Noreen gets enough credit for building the Greystone brand. She kept it all together, especially when Richard went into politics. However, she has been delegating more of the company's operations to the grandchildren. I guess she is semi-retired."

"My best friend Leo was recently put in charge of the Spice and Stone wine division. That was Richard's baby."

"Spice and Stone?" Cinnamon murmured.

"Greystone's flagship wine started nearly sixty years ago, was originally called Spice Stone wines. They produce aged, full-bodied wines with a rich blend of spices that give them a distinctive flavor. Richard was always passionate about the art of winemaking. You are in for a treat. The cabin has a wine cellar with wines from forty years ago."

Chapter Nine

Cabin was not the word she would use for the hulking stone building she could see in the car headlights as they drove up the paved driveway flanked by looming evergreen trees. It was a substantial two-story building with brick, stone, and wood elements. The front door was a heavy wooden door, and it seemed as if it had a wraparound porch. She assumed the views would be stunning in the day. The interior was equally impressive; she smelled the aroma of aged wood as soon as she stepped inside.

"Here is a flashlight," Jax said, handing her a big light. "I am just going to get all the supplies from the car. You can have a look around. I'll be back in a flash."

"It's cold up here," Cinnamon said, pulling her jacket closer. "Are you sure we are still in Jamaica?"

Jax laughed. "We are. I'll light a fire, and the place will get warmer in a flash." He left her to go to the car, and she looked around.

The interior revealed a blend of modern comforts and vintage aesthetics. The living room had plush leather sofas with blankets draped on each arm. She picked up one of them and covered her shoulders. "Now that was better."

A stone fireplace seemed to be the room's central focus; the furniture seemed like aged wood furniture. She guessed that they were probably antiques, but she wasn't knowledgeable about those things. She was impressed with the rugs, though; there had intricate patterns in shades of browns and oranges.

She moved from the living room into the kitchen, which had a blend of modern convenience and classic design. It boasted a large farmhouse table that could seat at least twenty people and a collection of copper cookware neatly arranged on the wall in four rows. How did she know that? She shone the light on them, and four rows gleamed in the half-light. All the pots here were copper. How did she know that? She was having a serious case of déjà vu.

She also knew that the grand staircase, which led to the second floor, had four bedrooms. She had stayed here before! How else would she know she could slide down the banister if cushions were placed all around and someone was there to catch her when she landed? Goodness, where did these memories come from?

She wandered down the hallway; there was a guest bathroom and a large study. She went behind the large wooden desk and drew the curtains. She only needed to tug on the middle one, and the whole thing slowly opened up. The moonlight illuminated the room, revealing shelves lined with old books and intriguing artifacts. A collection of wooden dolls would be at the bottom of the floor-to-ceiling bookcase. How did she know that?

Jax returned just as Cinnamon was shining the flashlight to confirm her suspicions. "Impressive, isn't it?" he remarked.

Cinnamon looked up. "Yes, it is."

"This was Richard's office, his favorite place in the house."

"This is going to sound really weird," Cinnamon frowned, "but were there wooden dolls on…"

"Oh, yes," Jax moved closer, "how did you know that? Richard had a collection of little wooden dolls. That was his hobby—wood carving. When he was done, he said his head was clearer, and he could get off the hill and be sane. He took them with him when he sold the place to me," Jax said. "He left a box of old photos, though. I have been meaning to give them to Noreen."

"Can I see them?" Cinnamon asked.

"Sure," Jax nodded. "Why are you so interested in Richard Greystone?"

"I feel as if I have been here before," Cinnamon said, "as a little girl."

"Oh," Jax raised an eyebrow. "We should explore that some more. I lit the fire in the hearth; you'll soon feel the warmth, and I have lots of food. My chef packed us enough food to feed an army. I told him to go with a mountain camp theme to impress you, of course."

Cinnamon laughed. "On tonight's menu is grilled salmon seasoned with secret herbs that only my chef knows. There's also a savory mushroom risotto and a medley of roasted vegetables that'll make your taste buds dance."

"And we have a decadent chocolate lava cake for dessert, oozing with warmth brand sweetness. Trust me, you won't want to skip it. And, of course, to wash it all down, I've got an impressive selection of wines or any other beverage of your choice."

"Oh, wow," Cinnamon whispered.

"But first, I need light," Jax laughed. "We do have

electricity. I just need to switch on the solar system. I wonder if the batteries are dead or if we have enough juice to power the lights until morning. The panel is in the laundry. I'll be back, little lady."

Cinnamon giggled. "What's that accent?"

"Cowboy, wild west."

She chuckled and headed back to the living room.

"Let there be light." He came back and flipped on a switch. The outside lit up. She could see the landscape better, with many hulking trees in the background. She also saw little details of the inside better; the rugs and cushions had mountain motifs in green and white. The plush settees were dark brown.

"Do you need any help?" Cinnamon asked.

"No, I have it all planned out," Jax said. "You had a tough week; I can handle this." He set the table, placed two fat electric candles in the center, and started taking out the food from the warmers. The aroma of the food filled the air. Cinnamon's stomach growled in response.

"What am I missing?" Jax asked. "Oh." he snapped his fingers. "Music. Don't go anywhere. I have a little portable CD player in the study."

Cinnamon chuckled, "You are going all out."

He came back with his portable CD player and pressed play. Enya's, Orinoco Flow came on.

"Oh, goody," Cinnamon clapped her hands. "Love it."

"I am happy you do because this CD is filled with Enya's greatest hits." Jax pulled out a chair for Cinnamon. "I hope you enjoy the meal, madam. It's not every day I get to host someone as special as you."

Cinnamon sat down. "This is perfect."

Jax smiled. No words needed to be said.

****

They hiked in the surrounding hills of the cabin. The morning was bleak so they chose an easy trail. It, too, felt familiar to Cinnamon. She didn't say that to Jax, though. She didn't want him asking questions about her familiarity with the place. She had a sneaky suspicion that she had been here before with her mom and Richard Greystone. Maybe this was their lovers' hideaway.

Why couldn't she remember anything more, though? She couldn't remember the people she was here with, just a lingering familiarity when she went to certain places.

The surrounding hills were beautiful, a mesmerizing combination of greens. The morning mist clung to the hills, lending an ethereal quality to the landscape. Cinnamon's thoughts swirled as she walked, captivated by the beauty of the hills but also haunted by the elusive fragments of her past.

She stole glances at Jax; he had a hint of a morning stubble, adding a little ruggedness to his handsome face. Being here with him right now just felt right. It's as if she had known him for centuries instead of days.

They stopped at the apex of the hill they had just walked up. They could see the cabin in the distance and other houses dotting the top of the various hills. It was indeed the perfect hideaway. Jax tucked her hands into his. "I never get tired of this view."

Cinnamon nodded. "I see why you like it. The air up here is so pure. I slept like a baby last night. I feel lighter, happier as if the city below us was tying me down somehow."

"That's exactly how I feel," Jax curled his fingers over hers. "We should come up here as often as we can. We are quite compatible, Cinnamon Cooper. I kissed you, and I knew." He turned to her and cupped her face in his hands. "But no kissing this weekend. We'll see how compatible we are outside of that."

Cinnamon smiled and reached up, kissing him briefly on his lips. "You are a breath of fresh air. I can't believe you are real."

"I could say the same thing about you," Jax smiled. "How is it that you have reached twenty-four, and I am the first one to kiss you? What's the catch? Do you turn into a seven-headed monster in the night?"

Cinnamon laughed. "No."

"The cat woman?"

"Oh no," Cinnamon laughed. "I think there is someone for everyone, and you just need to stand still, and you will find your person. I don't have to kiss all the frogs to find the one."

"I agree," Jax nodded.

Chapter Ten

They visited the wine cellar, where there was quite an extensive collection of wines. "How do the older wines taste?" Cinnamon asked, perusing the selection. "I think I read somewhere that wines are better in the five-to-seven-year range."

Jax nodded, "It depends on the winemaking process. Some wines are best enjoyed within the five to seven-year range, while others, especially those with more robust tannins and complex flavors, can benefit from extended aging. The older wines, well beyond a decade, offer a different experience altogether. They develop a maturity and depth that connoisseurs often appreciate."

"This one is fifty-eight years old; it is called the Rosemary Ruby. It's a rare gem. Richard's favorite," Jax explained.

Cinnamon gasped, "That's my grandmother's name."

"Maybe it's a coincidence," Jax said. "He named his wines from spices and stones."

"Hence the name Spice Stone wines," Cinnamon murmured. But something was not adding up. Her mother's name was Anise Crystal, her name was Cinnamon Jade, her sister's name was Cayenne Onyx, and her grandmother's name was Rosemary Ruby. What a weird coincidence. Something was odd here.

She wanted to point it out to Jax but thought better of it. She may sound crazy, and linking her grandmother to Anise Crystal wouldn't take a genius to put things together after that.

"Does he name other wines?" Cinnamon asked.

"Not many," Jax said. "The Rosemary Ruby is still the star in the Spice Stone series. There is also a Ginger Diamond and a Clove Amber. You know what, let me get the Clove Amber; you will love it. It has the warmth of cloves and a subtle amber hue."

Jax disappeared for a moment and returned with a bottle that seemed to glow in the ambient light of the cellar.

Cinnamon examined the label with interest. "Clove Amber, love the name."

"You'll love the taste, too," Jax grinned. "Let's go."

He poured a small amount into glasses when they reached the kitchen, the rich aroma of cloves wafted through the air.

"Richard had a way of connecting the essence of the spice with the character of the wine," Jax said, swirling the wine in his glass. "The Rosemary Ruby, for example, has a vibrant and robust profile, much like the herb itself. The Ginger Diamond has a certain sharpness and clarity to its taste."

Cinnamon tentatively sampled the Clove Amber and was pleasantly surprised by the complexity of the flavors. It didn't make her want to spit it out instantly. It was actually good.

"This is amazing," she murmured. "I am pleasantly surprised. I mean, I am no wine connoisseur, but I don't hate it."

Jax grinned, "Richard believed each wine should evoke an emotion, a memory, or a sense of place. It's not just about the taste; it's about creating an experience. Richard used to say wine is like storytelling; every bottle he created is a narrative waiting to be discovered."

Cinnamon nodded. "Well, I'll drink to that. To Richard Greystone."

"To Richard Greystone," Jax repeated. They clinked glasses together and drank.

****

It was quite a day. Jax taught her to play chess. They finished the bottle of Clove Amber, had some scrumptious food prepared by his chef, and took another evening hike. When they returned, Jax brought out the box of pictures he had saved for Noreen Greystone.

"I found it under his bed in the master bedroom," Jax said. "He probably forgot about it."

"Ah," Cinnamon opened the box in anticipation. There was a stack of pictures, mostly of the cabin and the surrounding areas. They were beautifully captured. Even though the photos were obviously old and fading somewhat, you could see the beauty.

She looked them over and handed them to Jax one by one.

"He had talent," Jax said, "some of these can be restored, blown up, and framed."

"I'd say," Cinnamon murmured.

And then there were the pictures of a young Richard with an afro. This must have been the sixties. Cinnamon laughed.

"He was quite handsome. He looks a little like that guy who sang, 'Down the way, where the nights are gay, And the sun shines daily on the mountaintop. I took a trip on a sailing ship, and when I reached Jamaica, I made a stop.'"

Jax grinned. "Harry Belafonte. Bet you don't know the words for the rest of the song."

"I do know it," Cinnamon said, "Harry Belafonte songs were what Grandma Sadie used for my bedtime songs. This and 'Island in the Sun' were bedtime staples."

"Oh really?" Jax said, "Let's test your memory."

They started singing together.

Cinnamon laughed helplessly as Jax whirled her around the living room to the imaginary music.

"This brings me back," Cinnamon said, sitting down. "Grandma Sadie was a Harry Belafonte fangirl."

Jax smiled. "You lived with your great-grandmother?"

"Yup," Cinnamon picked up the pictures again. "My great-grandma is still alive and pretty young for a great-grandma. She is seventy-eight this year. The women in my family procreate early."

"Tell me more," Jax urged.

"My mother had me when she was thirteen. She lived with Grandma Sadie for a while and then moved out at sixteen. Grandma Sadie was too strict and suffocating for her."

"What about her own parents?" Jax asked, "Where were they?"

"They were around…"

"What is it?" Jax asked.

"I er.." Cinnamon looked down at the picture in her hand. It was a picture of her grandmother, Rosemary Ruby, and her grandfather, Ronald Cooper, with Richard Greystone and Noreen. They were in tennis outfits. The Coopers were an obviously younger couple, but they all looked great together.

She knew how her grandparents looked when they were younger because of the wedding picture Grandma Sadie had at the back of the bookcase in her room. Cinnamon had once stumbled across it and taken it out of what she assumed was unintentional hiding.

Her grandmother had promptly put it back even further into her busy bookcase.

They looked a little bit like this. Rosemary's hair was long, thick, curly, and in a high top knot, and Ronald had an afro.

"You look like you've seen a ghost," Jax said.

"Well…" Cinnamon handed him the picture, "that's Richard Greystone, his wife, and my grandparents. You were just asking about them."

"Your grandfather's name was Ronald Cooper, and your grandmother is Rosemary Ruby Cooper?" Jax asked.

Cinnamon nodded. "I knew the wine, Rosemary Ruby, was not a coincidence."

"I'd say," Jax nodded. "I think Noreen's maiden name was Cooper."

"Is that so?" Cinnamon shook her head. "What a coincidence."

Cinnamon hastily flipped through the pictures to see if there were more. There were many more pictures, but none of the Greystones and the Coopers posing together. The remaining pictures were mainly of her grandmother in various poses. Most of her dresses were short, the style of the times, and she wore chunky platform shoes that emphasized her long legs.

Cinnamon smiled; she had been so pretty back in the day.

Jax took the photo of Rosemary in a short red dress and whistled, "Your grandmother was gorgeous."

Cinnamon nodded. "I want to be as desirable as her when

I grow up. You saw her at the restaurant; she's still hot."

There was writing on the back of the picture; it read, "Valentine's Day 1984, Love Always Rosemary."

Had she sent it to Richard? Cinnamon swallowed, hastily giving Jax the other picture so he wouldn't notice the writing on the back.

The one she hastily handed him was a picture with Rosemary pregnant, dated 1985. "It's a girl," was printed on the back.

The one she had in her hand was of a baby. On the back, it said, "Anise Crystal."

What on earth?

Cinnamon tucked the photo into the middle of the stack before Jax saw it.

She didn't know what to make of it. Were the Coopers and the Greystones family friends? Was Rosemary Richard's love interest, or was it Anise? Or was it Grandma Sadie?

What on earth was going on?

Who was Richard's love interest out of the three women?

Why did Richard name his wine Rosemary Ruby? It was clearly not a coincidence. It was his flagship wine, his first-ever wine in the Spice Stone series.

It was the exact same age as her grandmother. They obviously were not strangers; she signed one of her pictures, "Love, Rosemary."

And why was Rosemary sending pictures of her daughter Anise Crystal to him? And if they knew each other, why was Noreen taking Anise to court? And what of her own memories of this place?

When had she actually come here?

"I have some serious questions for my grandmother," Cinnamon murmured.

Jax looked at her. "They were probably family friends and

lost touch through the years; it happens."

"But what about the naming of his wine, Rosemary Ruby? It is the same age as Rosemary Ruby Cooper Landry, my grandma."

Jax nodded. "You have a point."

Cinnamon sighed. "Can I get the whole stack of pictures? Noreen has no use for them, or Richard wouldn't have left them here."

"Sure," Jax nodded. "Want to play another game of chess or bathe in the stream nearby?"

"In this coldness?" Cinnamon shook her head. "Chess it is."

Jax laughed. "And I think we should sample a bottle of Rosemary Ruby to take your mind off this puzzle."

"Oh yes. I am in," Cinnamon nodded.

Chapter Eleven

She couldn't think of anything else for the rest of the weekend; her mind churned with the mystery. She had even jotted down a timeline on a piece of paper this morning while Jax had gone fishing.

Richard Greystone had been eighty years old when he died; her grandmother Sadie Guthrie was currently seventy-eight, and she had never married. She had lived with Matthew Copeland until his death nearly thirty years ago.

When she was twenty, they had Rosemary Ruby Copeland together. That would have made Richard Greystone twenty-two at the time.

They were in the same age range. It was also the same year he started his wine company when Rosemary was born, and he named his flagship wine Rosemary Ruby.

Had he known of her? That was the big coincidence number one.

Another coincidence was the pictures of Rosemary with

her first husband, Ronald Cooper, Noreen, and Richard. Obviously, he knew her; they were friends, and they even played tennis together. And then there were the pictures of Rosemary alone. Those poses were sultry and suggestive; added to that, they were signed with love, now and always.

Was that romantic? It definitely felt that way.

And why did Rosemary name her daughter Anise Crystal, the same Stone and Spice theme that she was named herself?

Then, there was big coincidence number three. Richard left a significant portion of his money to Anise. Anise said sleeping with him would be gross. So what was the link? She needed the link!

Cinnamon fretted about it all the way back to Kingston.

She toyed with the idea of talking about it to Jax, but she held back.

"What's bothering you?" he asked; he had picked up on the fact that her brain was churning a mile a minute.

"I was thinking about my grandfather," she said, and that was the truth. Rosemary's first husband, Ronald Cooper, was in several pictures. It had been nice to see pictures of him. He was a handsome, fair-skinned, muscular guy; he looked like a catch back in the day.

It was the first time she had seen him besides that picture in Grandma Sadie's house. No one talked about him.

She didn't know his side of the family; she didn't know anything about him. It was nice to see him in other pictures.

"He died the year I was born."

"How did he die?" Jax asked.

"Suicide," Cinnamon sighed. "No one talks about him; my mother hisses like a feral cat if his name is mentioned. She goes as far as not talking to anyone with the first name. If your name is Ronald, she is ghosting you."

Jax glanced at her and then back on the road. "Are we

going to talk about what else is on your mind?"

"Like what?" Cinnamon looked at him.

"Like the fact that your mother is Anise Crystal," Jax said, "and you are afraid to tell me."

"You know?" Cinnamon gasped.

"It wasn't hard to figure out," Jax said. "I am shocked it took me two days to get to it. You look a lot like her. And there is the Spice and Stone motif in your names. It's hard to miss. I omitted to tell you this, but Richard had a wine in his private collection that has never been released called the Anise Crystal; it's thirty-eight years old. He sits in his study and drinks it and cries."

Cinnamon gasped.

"That's not all. Twenty-four years ago, he released a limited edition Cinnamon Jade. It's one of his best wines, in my opinion; it has notes of warm Cinnamon and then a cool mint. I brought back two bottles with me in the back. I wanted you to taste your namesake."

"I er…" Cinnamon didn't know what to say.

"Whatever went on with the women in your family and Richard Greystone had to be intense," Jax said. "He told me once that there was an event in his life that almost drove him mad and that it was all his fault."

"I wonder what that was," Cinnamon said.

"I don't know," Jax looked at her. "But whatever it is doesn't affect how I feel about you."

He squeezed her hand. "We can get through this, right? I think we have the makings of something strong."

"Oh, Jax," Cinnamon squeezed back his hand. "I think we do."

****

Long after he dropped her home and she sat in the dark living room, she felt that squeeze of reassurance. She picked up the phone to call her mother.

"Mom," Cinnamon said when Anise answered the phone. "How are you?"

"I am okay," Anise said. "How are you?"

She sounded low. Cinnamon hated to start questioning her about the past. She knew how Anise got when the past was mentioned.

"I went with Jax to his cabin in the hills."

"That's great," Anise said, "you finally have a boyfriend. I have always wondered if my example had completely messed you up."

"I didn't have time to be messed up by you," Cinnamon chuckled, "I lived with you when I was twelve and left at eighteen. When I lived with you, you were hardly home."

"True," Anise chuckled. "I was going through my traveling phase then. But I got you the best nanny money could buy; Mandy was a good nanny, right?"

"The best," Cinnamon said.

"And I never carried any men around you; most of them are predators anyway."

"There are good men around," Cinnamon said. "I called because I saw some photographs today at Jax's cabin. He bought it from Richard Greystone. I couldn't believe it; there were photos of Nana with Ronald Cooper when she was younger. I realize that you never talk about him."

"There is a reason for that," Anise said as if she were choking.

"Did you know that Richard Greystone has a wine named after Nana Rosie, you, and even me?"

"Yes," Anise growled.

"Why is it such a secret?" Cinnamon started talking faster;

she could practically feel Anise bristling over the phone.

"Ask Rosemary," Anise said, her voice clipped, "and while you are at it, never mention good men and Ronald Cooper in the same sentence again."

She hung up before Cinnamon could get a word in.

Her next call to Nana was just as unproductive. As usual, she answered the phone chirpily.

"Cinnamon, how are you, dear?"

"Nana, I didn't know you knew Richard Greystone so well," Cinnamon said. "I was up at his old cabin this weekend and found some pictures of you, and it was only this weekend that I found out that his signature wine in the Spice and Stone series is called Rosemary Ruby."

Her grandmother didn't speak for what felt like minutes.

"You found pictures?" She cleared her throat.

"Yes, there were quite a few of you; there was one with you, Richard, Noreen, and Ronald."

"Oh really?" Her grandmother's voice turned husky. "We knew each other eons ago."

"It looked to be more than that; "you signed your pictures with love now and forever."

"Goodness Cinnamon, that was so long ago. Do me a favor: Burn those pictures and forget about them. And please do not bother your mother with this," Rosemary said. "We were family friends. Things turned sour. I don't know why Richard saved those mementos. Another call is coming in, dear; we'll speak soon, bye."

She hung up. Cinnamon couldn't believe it. Her grandmother hung up on her! She called Grandma Sadie. Grandma Sadie was her only hope. Surely, if she knew anything, she would tell her.

"Cinnamon," she answered the phone; the sound of music was in the background.

"Where are you?" Cinnamon asked.

"Church function," her grandmother answered, "is everything okay?"

"Yes, just calling to ask you something."

"When are you coming to visit?" Sadie moved to a quieter spot. Cinnamon instantly felt guilty. She had last visited Grandma Sadie two months ago. She tried to go every month and spend all day with her, but work commitments had made her visits sporadic.

"Soon, grandma. Can I ask you something?"

"Sure," Grandma Sadie said.

"Do you know Richard Greystone?"

"Yes," Grandma Sadie said.

"Did you know he was friends with Nana Rosie?"

Grandma Sadie went quiet. "Cinnamon."

"Yes, Granny."

"Let bygones be bygones; leave the past alone."

"But Grandma, there is no leaving the past alone when Richard Greystone left Anise his personal fortune. Were they having an affair?"

"Hell no," Grandma Sadie said, "those are very distasteful accusations."

"Then why?" Cinnamon asked.

"Come by, we'll talk," Grandma Sadie said. "My other phone is ringing. Goodnight, dear."

"Goodnight, Grandma," Cinnamon said faintly. She didn't hear any other phone ringing, and since when did she have a second phone?

She had been stonewalled by the women in her family. Cinnamon snorted. What were they hiding? She couldn't wait until Cayenne got home. She had left a note on the fridge that she had gone to Alex for the day.

Cinnamon bathed, made some tea, and was about to watch

a movie to take her mind off the intrigue in her family life when Cayenne got home.

"You have to tell me everything," Cayenne said as soon as she walked in. "Did you do the deed and use up all of the condoms? How was it?"

"No, we didn't do the deed," Cinnamon shook her head.

"Oh," Cayenne made a face. "I was hoping for a juicy story."

"We had non-sexual fun, though," Cinnamon said. "I have a juicy story for you. I discovered that Jax bought the cabin from Richard Greystone, and I found this."

She handed the box of pictures to Cayenne and hovered over her as she looked through them.

"Oh my, this is Nana Rosie."

"Yes, our dear granny," Cinnamon nodded. "What do you think of it?"

"They were friends," Cayenne said.

"And?" Cinnamon raised an eyebrow.

"And, they were very, very good friends?" Cayenne shrugged. "I don't see where's the mystery."

"He named wines after us; his flagship wine brand is Spice and Stone. What do all of our names have in common?"

"Spice and stone?" Cayenne said doubtfully.

"Yes," Cinnamon nodded. "Think, lady. He is in pictures with Nana Rosie; he left his personal fortune to Anise. She grabbed the bottle of wine that Jax had given her. "What does this say?"

"Cinnamon Jade," Cayenne widened her eyes.

"I can remember playing up there when I was a kid!" Cinnamon shouted. "I was up there!"

"I don't remember that," Cayenne frowned.

"I was a baby. Maybe you weren't born yet. I am assuming I was there because Richard wanted to see me. I don't know.

I think we are related."

"You think he's your father for real?" Cayenne whistled. "My God!"

"I don't know how we are related," Cinnamon said. "He could be my great-grandfather, my grandfather, or my father. All of the women in the family tree above me could have had a run-in with him. I asked Anise about the pictures, and she hung up on me. I asked Nana Rosie about them; she sounded cross. I called Grandma Sadie; she said her other phone was ringing. Three generations of women in this family lying, obfuscating, and, in general, stonewalling me. I can't believe it."

Cayenne chuckled. "They are hiding something, and Anise is the weak link in that trio."

"Why Anise?" Cinnamon narrowed her eyes.

"She has the least experience in keeping secrets," Cayenne mused. "Grandma Sadie has seventy-eight years of secrets, all neatly compartmentalized and locked down. Nana Rosie is a fortress. She is probably worse than Grandma Sadie."

"I need to know," Cinnamon said. "So, how do I work on Anise?"

"You give her time," Cayenne smiled, "and when she least expects it, you visit her, bring her a bottle of her favorite wine, sit and chat, and then you pounce."

"Has that ever worked for you?" Cinnamon asked.

"Not always," Cayenne nodded. "But it's worth a try. You have to let her feel less cornered. Don't mention the pictures, the cabin, Richard Greystone, nothing."

"Okay," Cinnamon nodded. "I'll try that."

Chapter Twelve

It was amazing how three months flew by. Jax made every excuse to be around Cinnamon every day. He could have moved back to his office a long time ago but had stuck around just so that he could see her, watch her smile, and hear her voice.

He was a goner. Their connection deepened with each passing day, and it wasn't just about the physical attraction. He was captivated by how Cinnamon saw the world, her passion for life, and her strength in facing the challenges of her family's revelations. She was fast becoming his confidant. He was sharing dreams, fears, and everything in between with her. It was exhilarating and scary at the same time.

He was thinking forever, and he wanted to start right now.

He wouldn't see her as frequently now that his stint with Moretti Bedding was coming to a end. He had installed Kenneth as the co-manager with Marco, and Kenneth would report to him.

There was no need for him to stick around Moretti's anymore. The building was overhauled, additional staff were hired, and the parking lot didn't look like a junkyard anymore.

He was going to miss seeing Cinnamon every day. It was getting even more difficult to keep his hands off her and maintain his slow approach. He had never craved so much contact with a woman.

He needed to take the next steps, and that could be anywhere from asking her to move in with him to marriage.

He liked the permanency and commitment that marriage would bring. The idea that they would become one.

He was eager for that to happen. And he didn't think it was too soon. He had been in a relationship with Carissa for five years and never felt this urgency.

His phone rang.

"Can you make it for family dinner this evening, darling?" It was his mother. "Nelson and I have an announcement to make. And bring your girlfriend. I want to meet her."

Jax sighed; their honeymoon period away from family and friends was officially over. He didn't know how Cinnamon would handle this meetup. She was no closer to finding answers about her mother, Richard Greystone, or who her father was. And the women in her family were avoiding her questions. This would be throwing her straight into the lion's den. If this was a family party co-hosted by Nelson and his mom, then most of the Greystones would be there. He wondered if Cinnamon was up for it.

He would cowardly text her and then wait for her response. "Family dinner at my mom's tonight at seven. I hope you can make it."

She would be packing up to leave. It was Friday evening.

He spun around in his chair and looked down at the city skyline. His offices in the commercial offices of the Wilde Building had a view of the mountains and the city. He had not made it to the mountains in three months since they had last gone there together. He longingly looked at the undulating greenery in the distance.

"We could take a trip to the mountains after," he texted back. "Wake up to the sweet mountain air."

"Okay," she sent a mountain emoji. "Excited about the mountain part. Terrified about the dinner."

He texted back, "You'll be fine. My mom will love you."

A knock on his door had him looking up; it was Clive Green, his staff attorney, good friend, and shareholder in the Wilde Property Group of companies. When Jax had been in college for his first degree, Clive had just gotten his law degree. They met on campus in the school's admin office. They had both been waiting for documents and had struck up a conversation.

Jax had told Clive of his dreams to invest in properties, and Clive had done all his legal work for free. "I believe in you so much," Clive had said, "I want shares in exchange for work done. I'll draw up a contract."

He had been doing Jax's legal work ever since. He was a brilliant guy. He had negotiated contracts for multimillion-dollar deals, navigated complex legal landscapes with finesse, and played a pivotal role in the success of the Wilde Property Group.

Their professional relationship had evolved into a deep friendship, cemented by mutual trust and shared aspirations.

Clive was the definition of metrosexual. He was always sleekly dressed in tailored suits that accentuated his trim physique. He had perfectly coiffed dreadlocks with a slight sheen to them, and a subtle aroma of high-end cologne lingered in his wake as he stepped into the office.

"Good you are here," Clive said. "I just finalized the contracts for the St. Mary property; all our ducks are in a row. I spoke to Greystone's lawyers. They are satisfied with the terms."

"Good," Jax nodded, "thank you for your hard work."

"Here are the documents; go through them thoroughly and let me know if you are completely fine with everything. It's not too late to change things." Clive handed Jax the documents and sat across from him.

"My mother is throwing a birthday party for me tonight on the Roof Top, the very first party in the new Wilde building. You should stop by if you have nothing better to do."

"Last week was your fortieth birthday," Jax said. "and I gave you forty bottles of Rosemary Ruby from my vintage wine collection. I will never ask you to choose a present again. Your tastes are too refined."

Clive laughed. "Livvie and I busted out a couple for a dinner party we hosted, and would you believe it, people were asking me to give them a bottle to take home. I am offended at their audacity."

Jax chuckled. "You shouldn't have told them how many you had. I don't know if I'll be able to make it to your party, though; my mom is having a family get-together."

"Ah," Clive nodded, "she and Nelson will announce the wedding date."

"Maybe," Jax shrugged. "It will be Mom's fourth marriage, his third. I hope they last; they don't have good track records concerning relationships. If they don't last, I don't want any repercussions on the business side of things."

"Once he signs the contracts," Clive said, "there is no turning back. I wrote those documents with that in mind, even put it in a little clause."

"Good," Jax nodded.

"While we are talking about the Greystones," Clive said, "I heard from their legal department that they are launching a new wine called the Anise Crystal."

"They are?" Jax raised his eyebrows.

"So Leo didn't tell you?"

"No," Jax shook his head.

"Richard Greystone worked on it for years and wanted to launch it this year. He died before he could, and today, Noreen withdrew her lawsuit against Anise."

"Oh," Jax murmured, "I wonder what changed."

Clive chuckled, "Imagine if I had stuck things out with Anise; I would have been married to an heiress."

Jax laughed, "You were in a relationship with Anise Crystal."

"Oh yes," Clive nodded, "when she was twelve and I was fourteen. It was all innocent; we were each other's first love. I wonder what my mother will say now when she hears that Anise Crystal has her own wine and shares in the Greystone dynasty?"

"She'll say, 'That's nice,' and keep it moving," Jax smiled.

****

It was a short walk to the residential building next door. He had not bothered to drive. It was a golden evening, the sun casting long shadows across the pavement as it dipped below the horizon. He entered his building and crossed the foyer, the soft glow of the chandeliers casting a warm ambiance. The concierge nodded in greeting, and he headed to the bank of elevators.

"I haven't seen you for weeks now," Leo said behind him. "We haven't played squash in months."

Jax turned to him and smiled. "Do you want to play a game now? I am free."

Leo shook his head. "I can't. I have that dinner party our parents are throwing, and I have some things to do before heading out. The wine launch is taking up a lot of my time. It's been chaos and confusion at the office because of it. I need to tell you something in the strictest of confidence."

"What?" Jax raised an eyebrow, pretending he hadn't just heard the secret from Clive.

Leo looked around dramatically. "I'll say it in your apartment. I hope you are ready for Grandpa's wine launch, his best work yet, or that's what he has claimed. He warned us to proceed with the launch even if he was not around."

"When is it again?" Jax asked.

"Next week," Leo said. "It should be fun."

Jax nodded. "Well, I'll be there with my plus one."

"The new girl," Leo grinned. "I heard through the grapevine that you have a girl and are keeping her from us. What's wrong with her?"

"I am not keeping her from you." Jax pressed the elevator button for the penthouse floor. Leo stepped in with him. There were six penthouse apartments; Leo owned one of them. They were practically neighbors.

"So, tell me about her," Leo said. "Why the secret?"

"I am not keeping her a secret," Jax said. "We've just been spending a lot of time together without an audience. She's beautiful, smart, and funny. We share the same taste in a lot of things. I met her at Mom's latest perfume launch. I initially thought she was a model. Turns out she's an accountant, and she's working at Marco's company. I think I'm a bit obsessed with her. I have never felt this way. Kissing her is a journey on its own. I'm actually thinking of marriage, children, and happily ever after. I am thinking long term."

"This seems serious." Leo raised an eyebrow. "It's the first in thirty years I have heard you talk like this. You never used to wax poetic like this about Carissa!"

"I know," Jax mused. "I guess I am taking Richard's advice and moving with intent because I know she is the one."

"Oh," Leo looked at him. "I can't wait to meet her then."

"You will tonight," Jax smiled. "At our parents' big announcement. I can't believe you and I will end up being stepbrothers."

Leo smiled. "It was always in the cards for me to be in your life as some type of brother. I was almost your brother-in-law if you had married Carissa."

They exited into the hallway. Each penthouse had its own secure entrance. Jax used his keycard to open the door, revealing a stylishly decorated living space with floor-to-ceiling windows that offered a breathtaking view of the city skyline.

"So, what's the secret?" he asked.

"Grandpa swore me to secrecy a few months ago," Leo said. "I had no idea which wine he was working on as his great pièce de résistance, the crowning glory of his life, but he had to tell me because I am the head of the Spice and Stone line. I had to okay the label design and marketing strategy and plan the promo party. Back then, I was like, fine, nice name, and then he died, and then there was confusion, and now…"

Leo headed for the bar, a centerpiece in the elegantly decorated living room. The soft glow from the nearby city lights filtered through the windows, casting a warm ambiance. Jax joined him at the bar, pouring himself a drink as well.

"Confused about the wine or something else?" Jax

inquired.

Leo sighed, taking a thoughtful sip. "About everything, I guess. The name of the wine is Anise Crystal."

Jax nodded. "It doesn't surprise me. He had a limited edition of that one at the cabin. He would sit and drink it and cry. I always pretended I didn't see him crying. Now I wish I had asked questions."

Leo sighed. "He recorded a video for Grandma, and she got it today. She is withdrawing the lawsuit. I am thoroughly confused.

"There is a video that he will only allow to be released at the launch; his lawyers have that under lock and key as well. And get this: I am supposed to invite Anise Crystal as a guest of honor.

"How am I going to accomplish that? She doesn't answer any correspondence from the company. The lawyers have been trying to get a hold of her for months."

"I know someone who knows her pretty well," Jax said.

"Well, okay then." Leo's phone rang. He answered it and then looked at Jax, "Please help me get in touch with her; I will have to take this. I don't know why my dearly departed grandfather created so much drama.

"Oh, and whatever you do, do not mention the word Anise Crystal around my dad; he gets testy when he hears her name. That is also quite strange."

Chapter Thirteen

"**I**t was her second time at Devina Shae's house, but her first time being inside. Cinnamon had worn a red turtleneck dress with a little flare at the bottom. She had kept her makeup minimal, and her hair slicked back in a long ponytail.

"You look edible," Jax whispered in her ear while standing at the imposing front door. His breath made her shiver.

Cinnamon giggled. "Stop; I am about to meet your mom. I didn't meet her at the launch party because I spent all my time with you."

"My mom is cool," Jax said. "She is laid back." He punched the doorbell, and it opened almost instantly.

"Hello, my love!" Devina said brightly. She hugged Jax and then looked at Cinnamon, her eyes wide. "You look exactly like Anise Crystal. Has anyone ever told you that?"

"I, er… yes," Cinnamon nodded.

"She is a gorgeous woman!" Devina hugged her. "And so are you."

"Mom, this is Cinnamon Cooper. She came to your perfume launch a couple of months ago. That's how I met her. She also works at Moretti Bedding as an accountant."

"Ah," Devina smiled, "well, come on in. It's great to meet you, Cinnamon. Almost everyone is here already, in the family room. Nelson was running late, and we were just about to serve hors d'oeuvres.

"Some people are arguing politics, religion, and the latest news, and some of us who just want to be at peace are playing various board games. It's not a formal setup; make yourself at home and have fun."

Cinnamon felt instantly at ease. Devina was masterful at that, leading the way in her flowing kimono, her strides graceful and confident. Jax held her hand warmly and reassuringly. They followed Devina through the elegant foyer into the warm glow of the family room, where the air was filled with the tantalizing aroma of freshly prepared appetizers.

There were about thirty people in the great room scattered in groups. As they entered, the chatter subsided momentarily as eyes turned toward the newcomers. Devina proudly introduced Cinnamon to the gathering.

"Everyone, this is Cinnamon Cooper. She's Jax's girlfriend. She works at Moretti Bedding with Marco."

"Cinnamon has saved my business more than once," Marco waved, sitting in a chair with his son on his lap.

"And she's my bestie!" Ella said, getting up from her monopoly game and coming to hug Cinnamon.

"Don't hog all her attention, Ella," Devina joked. "We are all eager to get to know her."

Ella laughed. "Okay." Cinnamon breathed a sigh of relief. There were familiar faces.

"Let me introduce you around," Jax said after she and Ella

chit-chatted. "My friend Leo is dying to meet you. He is on the patio and waving me over every two seconds."

"You didn't say your girlfriend was a dead ringer for Anise Crystal!" Leo said as soon as they walked onto the patio. "I had to do a double take."

Jax smiled. "Cinnamon, meet Leo Greystone, my oldest and best friend."

They shook hands.

"It's lovely to finally meet you," Leo said. "I should have known that Jax was hiding you from us because he didn't want competition for your affections."

Cinnamon smiled.

"Or he didn't want us to know that he is fraternizing with the enemy," a lady said drolly from a chair near them.

Cinnamon hadn't realized two persons were sitting there— an older lady and a younger one. They both looked familiar like she had seen them somewhere before. She couldn't place where.

"That's Carissa, ignore her," Leo said.

"No, don't ignore me," Carissa got up. "Who are you to Anise Crystal? And why did Jax take you to a family gathering when he knows how dangerous you are to my family?"

Cinnamon took a step back into Jax's arms. Carissa was advancing on her slowly like she was about to do her harm, a hateful glare in her eyes.

Jax wrapped his hand around her. "Carissa, back off."

Carissa stopped and looked behind her. "Can you believe this, grandma?"

"Barely. You are acting quite jealous, and I know it's not on my behalf."

The lady got up, tall and elegantly dressed in a manner that seemed timeless. Her silver hair cascaded down her shoulders, and her piercing brown eyes hinted at mischief. She assessed the situation with a subtle smile, an air of confidence surrounding her.

"Well, who do we have here?" she remarked, her voice a mix of amusement and curiosity. "Jax, my dear, it's lovely to see you defending your date from the viciousness of your jealous ex."

Carissa snorted. "I am not jealous of Jax. I just don't want to see him happy with a pretty girl and looking in love and content. I want him lonely and dejected so that I can feel better."

"Always honest to a fault," Jax chuckled. "Cinnamon, meet Carissa Greystone, my ex-girlfriend, and her grandmother, Noreen Greystone, my honorary grandmother."

Cinnamon held out her hand to Carissa, who shook it and gave her a smile. "Sorry about earlier."

When she extended her hand to Noreen, she hugged her instead. It was so unexpected. She was enveloped in a cloud of perfume.

"You sweet, sweet girl," Noreen pulled away from her and studied her face. "It's a pleasure to meet you as an adult, Cinnamon. You were such a pretty little girl, a chubby-cheeked little munchkin."

Everyone gasped. Cinnamon knew her mouth was open. Noreen knew her as a baby?

Noreen stood before her. "Your grandmother, Rosemary Ruby, was my sister-in-law."

That made sense, Cinnamon mused; Jax had said her maiden name was Cooper.

"Oh snap," Leo murmured beside her. "Rosemary Ruby is a person?"

"She is," Noreen smiled. "My youngest brother Ronald was married to her for twelve years. We threw the wedding in the backyard at our house. When Rosemary had Anise, I was the one who named her Anise Crystal. Then our families were fractured because of the accusations, but that's another topic for another time."

"You named my mom?" Cinnamon whispered.

"Yes, I did," Noreen nodded. "Richard even had a limited edition wine made in her honor. Just a thousand bottles."

"Wait up," Carissa was the one who spoke, echoing all their thoughts. "What? Grandma, weren't we taking Anise Crystal to court?"

"Not anymore," Noreen said. "I was operating under the assumption that Anise was not a Greystone. I was mistaken. Your grandfather left me a video. And what a video it was. I wish he could have told me what was in it when he was alive. Anise would have had her rightful place in this family, and you, my dear Cinnamon Jade, would have been welcomed and cossetted by the Coopers with open arms because you are my family, too."

"I don't understand," Cinnamon whispered.

"I know," Noreen said. "Unfortunately, your grandmother and mother's story is not my story to tell. Apart from being not privy to certain details, I just found out today what really happened in the past. Richard made a video he wanted to share with all the family and shareholders. I don't want to preempt that. Hopefully, you and your sisters will be there for it."

Leo nodded. "I have been trying to get in touch with Anise, but to no avail. She doesn't answer company mail."

"I'll talk to her," Cinnamon said huskily.

"Well then, let's not be wet blankets," Noreen said brightly. "I think your parents are going to announce a date for their marriage. I hope to God this is their last one."

****

"It had been quite an evening. Jax's family, the Greystones—everybody had been nice except Nelson Greystone, who glowered at her all evening. He and Devina had announced their marriage date. It was to be a New Year's Day ceremony in Nelson's backyard. But she had so many questions lingering about her side of the family; it was driving her slightly mad.

She admitted as much to Noreen, who came over to talk to her several times during the evening.

"You know what," Noreen said, "let's take a picture. Send it to them, caption it 'family' with a question mark, and see what happens. We need to grin really wide."

They did just that.

They took the picture, and she sent it to Anise and Nana Rosie.

"Did they respond?" Jax asked when she got in the car.

"I just hit send," Cinnamon grinned.

"That went well," Jax said. "Everybody seems to like you."

"Yes, they were really nice," Cinnamon smiled. "Your mother was shocked to hear that Cayenne was my sister."

Her phone pinged.

"Your house at ten tomorrow," Nana Rosie texted first. "I'll make sure your mother joins us."

Cinnamon laughed. "Finally! Sending them the picture really worked."

Jax smiled at her exuberance. "Who bit first?"

"Nana Rosie. She said she'll bring Mom to my place at ten tomorrow."

"Which means I won't pick you up until about twelve?"

Jax said.

"Twelve is good," Cinnamon nodded.

"There is this restaurant in the hills that sells the best-curried goat in the world," Jax said. "I'll make a reservation."

"And I am looking forward to it," Cinnamon said.

****

Jax got home a little before eleven after dropping Cinnamon off at her house. He was too keyed up to sleep. Tomorrow was the day he was going to propose to Cinnamon. He loved her, and he didn't want a long engagement. He didn't want to wait nearly thirty years until she came to her senses, as Nelson had said, nor did he want them to be perpetually engaged like he had been with Carissa. Unlike that relationship, he was sure about this one.

There was karaoke going on in the residents' lounge. One of the residents was singing 'Forever Young.' Normally, Jax would join, but he spotted Nelson staring down into a glass of wine at the bar area.

That was odd; Nelson rarely spent time at his apartment in the Wilde Building. He had been an investor, but he had so many other homes. When he had reserved an apartment for himself here, Jax had never thought he would use it for personal reasons. He sat beside Nelson at the bar.

"I thought you would be in bed with my mom now. You two just announced your happy news," Jax said.

"She broke up with me," Nelson replied.

Jax widened his eyes. "Why?"

"I told her something," Nelson inhaled, "and then we had a blazing row."

"Oh," Jax said. "I can't take sides here."

"I know," Nelson said. "We'll sort this out. This isn't our

first row. I mean, I expected the blow-up. I told her she drove me crazy when she married that last guy. I thought that would have been our time, and then I told her I even dated Anise Crystal in desperation to get her attention."

"I didn't know that," Jax said. "At this point, it seems as if Anise has dated all the men in the one percent."

Nelson laughed. "I didn't have sex with her, never got a chance to. My dad found out about us and lost his mind. I had never seen him so angry. It was epic. Anise never called me back after our first date. I guess Dad got to her? I don't know what they had."

"The latest wine is dedicated to her," Jax said.

"I heard," Nelson nodded.

"Jax! Nelson!" It was Livvie Green, Clive's wife. "Clive's party is still going on upstairs; you both must show your faces."

"I forgot about that," Jax murmured. "I am coming right behind you, Livvie!"

"You go ahead," Nelson said. "No, wait. I have been trying to poach Clive from you for ages. I want him on my legal team. He's a savant at his craft."

Jax laughed.

Chapter Fourteen

Cinnamon heard raised voices downstairs as soon as she woke up. Her mother and grandmother had obviously arrived. She put the pillow over her head. Her nana had said ten o'clock.

She pulled off the pillow and looked at the clock; it was a little past eight.

"Cinna! Cayenne yanked the door open. I know you can't sleep with the ruckus downstairs. You have to come down before they kill each other."

Cinnamon took the pillow from her ears.

"Apparently, Nana Rosie wanted to meet here at ten, but Anise wanted to sneak in before and tell you her story. And to tell you the truth, I wouldn't mind hearing what you did to get the two of them over here so ready to talk."

"I sent them a picture of me and Noreen Greystone and captioned under it 'family' with a question mark."

"Oh," Cayenne smiled. "Is she family?"

"She was our grandfather's sister."

"Oh," Cayenne nodded. "That would explain the pictures. Come on, I can't wait to hear the story. Get up, girl."

"Okay, I'll be there in a bit. Please act as a referee until I get there."

"Sure," Cayenne nodded.

She hurriedly showered and got dressed. Her mother and grandmother were at opposite ends of the living room, snarling at each other. Cayenne was sitting between the two of them, her eyes wide.

"Good morning, family!" Cinnamon said breezily.

"Good morning," Anise and Rosemary grumpily replied.

Cayenne got up. "Am I glad you could join us. Does anybody want breakfast? Eggs, porridge, popcorn."

"Wine?" Anise asked.

"Not so early in the morning," Rosemary said. "I am surprised you are even up at this hour."

"I do yoga in the mornings," Anise said. "And then I meditate. I didn't get to meditate because of your message, so I am agitated."

"Then drink some coffee to calm yourself down," Rosemary snarled.

"Coffee doesn't calm people down," Cayenne said. "Doesn't it do the opposite?"

"It works for Anise; she has ADHD," Rosemary said.

"Since when?" Both Cinnamon and Cayenne asked, with varying levels of incredulity in their voices.

"Since she was diagnosed around nine," Rosemary said. "She also has other disorders, which I am sure names haven't been coined for yet. Why do you think she is like this? She has difficulty sticking with anything; she flits from partner to partner. She has difficulty concentrating on one thing, is overly emotional, lies sooner than tell the truth, and's an attention-seeking person…"

"I am overly emotional because you are underemotional," Anise rebutted. "And I may be many things, but I am not a liar!"

"And she doesn't want to take her medication or get treated," Rosemary added.

"I am fine. I don't have ADHD as badly as Rosemary wants me to have it," Anise snorted. "I think she wants me drugged up and comatose to run my life. She is evil like that. She likes to think I have some sort of illness to excuse how she treats me."

"Good lord," Rosemary whispered. "Can we be in the same room for five minutes without hearing how evil I am?"

"No," Anise said. "You should hear it every day."

Rosemary sighed and looked at Cinnamon. "Now, the reason why I am here so early…"

"Lies!" Anise said.

"I did not give my reason yet," Rosemary said calmly.

"My mother called me and told me not to speak to you about what really happened. She wanted to keep the secrets going," Anise said. "I was supposed to come over here and tell you the sanitized version of my life to perpetuate the lies already told."

"She doesn't want you to know the truth because she knows she won't be portrayed well. Her lies are why I am like this. Her lies ruined me! I am ruined!"

"Oh, stop with the theatrics, Anise. The sanitized version is the real version. You refuse to acknowledge the truth and get help for your mental disorders. You genuinely believe the make-believe version of your life. I am flabbergasted."

"Argh!" Anise squealed. "You see why I don't talk to her regularly. She loves to say in her perfect little radio voice that I have a mental problem!"

Rosemary sighed. "You do have issues. I thought you had at least outgrown some of them by now."

Cinnamon moved further into the room and sat down. Anise had a stubborn cast on her face. She got up and started pacing the floor from the back door to the front. How often had she seen Anise do this through the years? Too many times to count. It was as if she couldn't sit still for long periods of time or focus on any one thing to save her life.

She did have ADHD; it explained so much about her.

Cayenne handed her the coffee, and she paused long enough to drink it. It literally calmed her down. Cinnamon had never seen coffee work like that before. Anise's face took on a determined mask.

"Cinnamon deserves to know who her father is, and I will tell her. I know how much it hurts not to know the truth," Anise said softly.

"Before you tell your version of the truth," Rosemary sighed, "I should tell my side at least."

Anise didn't acknowledge her mother. She carried her cup to the kitchen and then returned and sat down.

Cinnamon didn't know if she drew a breath. Cayenne put the popcorn in the microwave and came to stand at the kitchen doorway. She, too, didn't want to miss a word. Nobody spoke. Rosemary looked down at her hands, only rousing herself when the microwave pinged. Cayenne seemed reluctant to go for her unusual breakfast.

"I had an affair with Richard Greystone," Rosemary said softly.

Cinnamon sat up straighter.

"He was my mother's friend from back in the day. They were all from the same neighborhood in St. Ann. He was the young businessman who made good. I came to Kingston for college, and my mother told him to look out for me."

"That's it?" Cinnamon asked skeptically. "Why were you named Rosemary Ruby like his wine?"

"He always talked about naming his first wine Rosemary Ruby. My mother said she liked the sound of it, so she borrowed it. His name came first, though I and the wine arrived in the same year."

"Oh," Cinnamon exhaled.

"Anyway," Rosemary inhaled shakily, "when I came to Kingston, he took me places. I hung out with his family, his wife Noreen, and Noreen's brother, Ronald. They were nice to me. He and Noreen were having problems long before I came on the scene. We started spending time together alone, and we fell in love. He offered to divorce Noreen. She refused. She knew he had fallen for someone but didn't know it was me. She said she wasn't letting him go; there were too many ties, the business and the children. And so Richard said we should stay away from each other. He didn't want to cheat on her.

"We stayed away from each other. I dated other people, including Ronald Cooper, Noreen's brother. I just never loved any of them. Not at the time. I was so caught up in Richard's spell.

"And then one weekend, there was a storm warning. Students who were living on campus were told to evacuate. Richard came for me. He was going to take me home, but the weather got bad fast, so he took me to his Kingston apartment. We finally gave in to our desires and spent the weekend together. That's when Anise was conceived. It's not like we had some long-running affair. When Richard learned about the pregnancy, he nudged Ronald to marry me.

"Ronald knew I was already pregnant when we married, and he knew the baby was Richard's. He just never cared.

He was a loving and caring guy."

Anise snorted. "Loving and caring my foot."

"Are you going to let me finish?" Rosemary asked.

"Go ahead," Anise shrugged.

"Nobody knew what the situation was except for the three of us. Noreen was happy that I had married her brother. She was a fantastic sister-in-law."

"She said she named Anise," Cinnamon said.

"Yes, she did," Rosemary nodded. "It was among the names in contention for a wine that year. I think they even had a limited quantity done in honor of Anise. Noreen thought Anise was her first niece, and Richard, Ronald, and I were happy to go along with the fiction."

"Oh," Cinnamon said, "that makes sense."

"Everything was peachy with us," Rosemary sighed, "until Ronald told her that Anise wasn't his biological child. She asked me who her father was; I refused to tell her, and then she started pulling away from me.

"Anyway, as the years passed, Ronald was promoted in their company. We were thriving as a couple and a family. It was just the three of us, and then I got pregnant when Anise was around eight.

"She totally lost it. She threw tantrums, craved attention on a scale that I did not think was normal, didn't listen, and was increasingly distant. It seemed like the news of my pregnancy had triggered a profound change in Anise, and I struggled to understand the sudden shift in her behavior.

"As my belly grew, so did the emotional distance between us. She deliberately tried to sabotage my pregnancy. I won't go into details, but it's because of Anise that I lost the baby."

"You slid down the stairs. It had nothing to do with me," Anise snorted, "she has blamed me for that ever since. That's when she turned cold and witchy and didn't care what happened to me after she lost her precious baby. I need more coffee to tell you this."

Cayenne got up and handed her another mug.

Anise took a sip and inhaled. "Okay, where was I?"

"Nana got pregnant, married Ronald Cooper, and then when she got pregnant again, she turned cold," Cinnamon said.

"Yes, that's right," Anise nodded, "my mother starved me of attention and had Ronald Cooper, the creep, pick up her slack, I thought he was my father, but nobody thought to tell me that he wasn't. Do you know those little books with pictures that children like to be read before bed?"

Cinnamon nodded. "I think so."

"Well, those weren't the stories Ronald Cooper read to me. His books were filled with naked people doing things to each other. He'd read them, then he'd touch himself, and he'd touch me. I told my mother about it the first time it happened. She was shocked. I could see that she didn't believe me, but she said, don't worry about it; I'll take care of it."

"The moment you told me he stopped reading to you," Rosemary said. "I knew you were setting him up."

"Oh no, he still read to me. When you were home, it stopped, but when you weren't…." Anise took a gulp of her coffee, "it was hell."

"I never left you alone with Ronald after that," Rosemary said. "Something within me knew you were going after him. I could feel it. So when I went away on business trips, I arranged for you to stay with Marjorie, our neighbor."

"And Ronald used to circumvent that by picking me up from school and telling Marjorie he would bring me by later. She didn't know what was happening, so she never protested." Anise said. "There was the one time you left for a reggae show; she was the MC and spent the entire weekend. Ronald didn't even bother to take me to Marjorie; he raped me for the whole weekend."

Cinnamon closed her eyes. Cayenne gasped.

Rosemary snorted in disbelief.

"And that's the time I ran away," Anise said. "He locked me in the house, but I escaped, jumped from the second floor—almost killed myself. I had to stay with people they didn't know because he would have come for me if I stayed with any of their friends. He knew how to pretend to be a good dad in front of people. Luckily, a friend hid me in his room for a few weeks. His mother eventually found me. I told her what happened and why I was hiding in her house like a fugitive, and she called the police."

Anise sighed. "The police called Child Services, and little old me got my own case worker and everything. They heard my story and put me in a group home with other troubled girls."

Anise inhaled. "I don't know why Rosemary and her husband came for me afterward. I would have been better off in that space. But they came, told the case worker that I had mental problems, and they had proof; Rosemary had me in therapy for my so-called ADHD.

"Ronald convinced them that I was an imaginative girl who wanted to have sex with my little boyfriend, and that's why I ran away.

"And the Child Protection Agency people sent me straight back to hell. Why wouldn't they? My father was a VP at Jamaica's leading winery, and my mother was Rosemary Ruby, the most famous voice on the radio. They were solid middle-class people who lived in a nice neighborhood. Why would they molest their daughter?

"My so-called case worker told me that I hurt my parents

when I do these antics. Antics!" Anise squealed. "I hate the word antics to this day! And my smug mother sat there and nodded, agreeing with them, and backed her husband. It's as if she wanted me to suffer."

"Let me interject here," Rosemary said. "I didn't back Ronald; I kept my mouth shut because that little boy was your boyfriend, and you were always imaginative. I wanted to hear the true story first.

"Anise, you are not a reliable source. Maybe I would have believed you if you had not been prone to telling stories and making up lies."

"When did I tell people fiction and make up lies?" Anise asked. "Give me one example."

"You told people that I locked you up in the basement and didn't feed you," Rosemary said. "That's the most blatant one. The teacher who you told was appalled."

"But you did lock me in the basement and starved me," Anise said.

"I closed the door to your music room, which was in the basement. The lock got stuck, and we had to call a locksmith. When freed less than an hour later, you refused to eat what the housekeeper had prepared.

"You embellished and exaggerated things all the time when you were a kid. I was not about to jump on Ronald's case without a fair hearing just on your say so."

"I just remember you weren't backing me," Anise said. "Ronald dropped me off at school the day after Child Protection Agency brought me back and threatened me on the way to school. 'Don't you dare tell anybody,' he said.

"So I ran away again. This time, when I did, I made sure I would not be found. No one would think to look for me in the tenement yards in Tivoli. The housekeeper had family there, and she was sympathetic to my plight. So I stayed in

Tivoli."

"I almost went out of my mind with worry," Rosemary said. "I didn't know where she was. That's when I clued Richard in about what was happening; he was devastated when he heard. We had agreed not to keep in touch after I married Ronald. He didn't interfere in our lives, and that was fine. When I told him that Anise was missing, it was quite a blow for him."

Anise made a rude sound.

"You do not appreciate that I cared," Rosemary said. "You still don't get how much I care for you deeply."

"If you had cared for me deeply," Anise snarled, "you wouldn't have allowed that pervert back in the house with me. You made him carry me to school. You pushed your head deep in the sand, thinking it would disappear.

"I married a pervert, too. The moment I found out about Paul; I almost killed him. I wouldn't let him within an inch of my children after that. That's what mothers do! They defend their young! They listen to their children! They don't make excuses. They act immediately!"

"How come I knew that was what I instinctively had to do? Even though you claim I have a mental disorder. Where were your instincts, and you are perfectly sane? You have always been terrible, cold, and detached."

Rosemary closed her eyes. "You will never understand the difficulties of dealing with a child like you, Anise. You have mental health problems, you could not distinguish real from fake, and you made things up. I still, to this day, don't know if you know the difference. That's why I insist on being around when you tell your story!"

The silence was deafening.

Anise looked at her mother in stony anger.

Cinnamon glanced at Cayenne. The two of them were

wide-eyed.

Cinnamon almost expected Anise to leave after such a revelation. But she took another swig of her coffee.

"I found out I was pregnant shortly after running. The people I was staying with all worked the streets. They suggested I do it too to make money to survive. Sex work was easy. One of them told me, you have a pretty face, and you are already sexually abused. At least this time, you'll be paid."

"So, at thirteen, I started working the streets. I wasn't really showing, even at six months. I was standing at the corner at one of our regular spots when the sun was about to set, and a fancy car drove up to my spot. I automatically went into work mode. Anise grimaced. An older man wound down the back window and said, "Good god, what have we done.""

Anise sighed; he told me to get in.

"I got in."

He said, "Anise Crystal, your mother sent me to find you."

"I started shaking. No, I said, "I don't want to go home to them.""

"Everything is going to be all right," he told me reassuringly. He took me to a doctor's office to get checked over, and then he made a phone call.

"I was sitting next to him when I heard him say to someone on the phone, Ronald, I found Anise. She's pregnant. You have three options: be charged with statutory rape and be left to the mercy of the state, I send someone to kill you now, or you kill yourself. You have until six o'clock to decide.

"Next thing I know, Ronald Cooper committed suicide. Shot himself in the mouth."

"Serve him right," Cayenne whispered.

"When I heard the news, that's exactly what I said," Anise snickered. "Anyway, Richard took me to Grandma Sadie's house because I was not going back to live with Rosemary Ruby ever again.

"If I never saw her face again, it would have been quite fine by me. I have always thought that Richard Greystone was a kind, compassionate man, the only one who listened to me when I needed someone to believe me the most.

"He gave me his number and said I should call him whenever I had a problem. I called him, and we would chat. It was mostly me venting. He would listen and make suggestions. He was the best example I had of a father figure.

"I even took you up to his cabin sometimes, Cinnamon," Anise said, "when you were a little girl. Noreen used to join us occasionally. She was quite nice, warm, and motherly. Richard told her about the falling out with my mom. I think she tried to make up for that.

"I had no clue that he was my father. Not even a hint of a clue. I just thought he was a grandfatherly type who had been friends with Rosemary and Ronald from back in the day. He only told me the truth when I started dating Nelson Greystone eight years ago."

"You dated Nelson Greystone," Cinnamon gasped. "He's your brother!"

"But I didn't know that. He didn't know either. I doubt he knows that I am his sister to this day. I left him as soon as I heard. Luckily, we weren't serious; I found him goofy and genuinely wondered what I was doing with him." Anise shrugged. "When I found out that I was Richard's daughter, I was shocked, pleasantly surprised, and quite frankly relieved because I thought we had the same father, Cinnamon, and it seriously grossed me out. I was going to tell you on your birthday. I wanted to tell you the whole story when my dear mother said I shouldn't. She was still in denial over Ronald

Cooper and still thinks I am lying.

"I agreed not to say anything to you or the public if she paid all of your tuition fees through college and if she gave you this townhouse."

Cinnamon glanced at Rosemary. "I thought you gave me the townhouse out of the goodness of your heart, Nana."

"I did," Rosemary said with a wry smile. "I also did not want Anise to broadcast our business in the streets. It was a fair exchange for some peace of mind. Now Richard has left her his inheritance and blown up this whole thing in our faces. After years of keeping secrets, he just upended the whole thing.

"What is it about people that when they feel their life slipping away, they don't care to keep the secrets they had emphasized you keep? What he did is pretty selfish, really. On leaving Anise his money, he, in essence, will force us to go public."

"He was a good man; I wish I had grown up with him and Noreen. I figure she was suing me because she has no idea what a convoluted story she was a part of."

Anise finished the coffee and held it up to the light. "This was good."

"So, to be clear, my father is Ronald Cooper?" Cinnamon asked faintly.

"Yes," Anise nodded. "If you want to know about his side of the family, you'll have to ask Noreen. She's your aunt. I hope now that you've heard what happened, you'll appreciate that I am unwilling to talk about him or see any pictures of his face again."

Cinnamon nodded. "I understand."

"Well, that's it," Anise stood up. "I am going to crash in Sage's bed. I suddenly have no energy. This part of my life is always draining. It's getting better, though, since I've been in therapy."

"Okay, thanks, Mom," Cinnamon whispered.

Cayenne hadn't touched her popcorn.

Rosemary waited until Anise went upstairs. "We don't know who your father is, Cinnamon. I can't be convinced to this day that Ronald Cooper was a pedophile. He was the stricter parent of the two of us, and Anise hated that."

"I went into depression when I lost my second pregnancy, and yes, I did blame Anise. I can't prove that she deliberately set me up to fall, but I know she was exceedingly happy when I did."

"Ronald literally picked up the parenting slack that year during my depression. Anise started accusing him of reading her dirty stories when he found her with pornography in her room. She ran away to stay with Clive Green, a minor at the time, and the only reason he didn't get in trouble and why child protection services didn't intervene further."

Rosemary inhaled. "Richard chose to believe Anise because he didn't know her, didn't know what we were dealing with. He couldn't fathom that she was telling lies; he thought he would just swoop in and do something for the little girl he had ignored up to that point. Poor Ronald. He killed himself because he knew Richard Greystone was not to be messed with, and he didn't stand a chance with Anise sounding so convincing."

Rosemary sighed. "I overcame my infatuation with Richard and grew to love Ronald. Anise never liked him; it's as if she knew he wasn't her biological father. She hated him from when she was just a tot, and he put up with everything."

"If you want to be sure who is telling the truth, you can do a DNA test with Noreen," Rosemary said, "or Calvin Green; he is Jax Wilde's lawyer, so you don't have to look too far. He was her little boyfriend. I think they were having sex.

With Anise, you never know."

Cinnamon gasped.

Rosemary sighed, "As for Anise being a prostitute, that never happened. Our old housekeeper, Vanessa, did help her to hide, but her sisters, who Anise stayed with, were street vendors; they sold ground produce at the side of the road. They bought her story that she was being raped, and they took care of her. That's where Richard found her at their stall downtown."

"I can't believe this," Cinnamon murmured.

"As for your father, Cayenne," Rosemary said, "I did my best to warn him about Anise; he never listened. And now he is in jail for absolutely nothing. Do you remember ever being inappropriately touched by Paul?"

"No," Cayenne said. "I just heard that I was molested and accepted it was so. I was just three."

"Well, he got twenty years of prison because of Anise's lies and paranoia," Rosemary sighed. "Your mother, unfortunately, lives in her own little made-up world, and once she convinces herself of something, it's hard to convince her differently. Be thankful you never interacted with her much while growing up."

Rosemary left.

Cayenne walked her to the door.

She slid all the way down to the floor after closing it. "Can you speak?" she asked Cinnamon after a while.

"I think so," Cinnamon whispered. "Who should I believe?"

Cayenne looked dazed. "If Noreen is your aunt, then Nana Rosie is the delusional one, defending her deceased husband at the expense of her child. She caused a world of hurt by not believing Anise. If this guy Clive Green is your father, then Nana Rosie is right, and our mother is a convincing storyteller and messed up at great levels."

"Or both things could have happened," Cinnamon said. "Ronald Cooper could have raped Anise, as well as Anise could have had a boyfriend who she was having sex with. The ladies she stayed with downtown could have sold ground produce as well as their bodies.

"Whatever the true story is, I am no closer to discovering who my father is or what really happened in the Cooper household."

Chapter Fifteen

Cinnamon couldn't wait to talk to Jax and ask his opinion.

"Boy, do I have a tall tale to tell you." She said as soon as she got into the car.

Jax smiled. "I am all ears." He listened with total incredulity through it all and then frowned. "Wow, I mean, wow."

"So what should I do?" Cinnamon asked. "Whose story should I believe?"

"I don't know what to tell you," Jax said. "I would test both Noreen and Clive. Let me call Clive and find out if he could be a possibility. This is intriguing."

He stopped at the side of the road overlooking a stream; they were in the foothills of the Blue Mountains. It was chilly already, so Cinnamon pulled on a sweater.

Clive answered Jax groggily. "Clive," Jax said, "I am sitting beside Cinnamon Cooper, my girlfriend."

"Oh, that's a pretty name," Clive chuckled. "I am not

jealous. I am sitting beside my wife, we are having Saturday brunch. We will be topping that off with a bottle of Rosemary Ruby."

"You are steadily going through the stash, huh?"

"Yup, the best birthday present ever," Clive chuckled.

"I told you my girlfriend's name, hoping it would ring a bell," Jax said. "She is Anise Crystal's daughter. You said Anise was your first girlfriend."

"Oh man, it's a small world," Clive said. "I remember the name Cooper now. Ronald Cooper was a piece of work."

"He was?" Jax asked.

"Yes," Clive said, "no offense to your girlfriend, but he was the worst piece of…ehem," he cleared his throat. "He molested Anise for years. She would tell me about it."

"Did you have a sexual relationship with her too?" Jax asked.

"No!" Clive said, offended. "We were innocent girlfriend and boyfriend, hold hands and hug kind of thing. Besides, I felt sorry for Anise; she had it rough at home with her dad. The things he did to that girl. I hid her once for days at my house one summer. When my mother found out, we continued hiding her for weeks."

"Do you believe him?" Cinnamon asked when Jax hung up the phone.

Jax nodded. "I do."

"Well then, there goes my grandmother's little theory," Cinnamon sighed.

"It sucks not to listen to your children," Jax said, "and it sucks to keep secrets."

"I can't wait to speak to Noreen," Cinnamon nodded. "I would really like to do that DNA test for my peace of mind and to exonerate my mother."

Jax clasped her hands in his. "You know what, let's do it. I can take you to her house right now. We can always visit the mountains at another time."

****

Noreen Greystone's house was in the hills of Kingston and was quite close to where Jax's mother lived. Cinnamon had called ahead, and she was home. Jax left her at the entrance so that she could have her private time with Noreen.

"You don't need an audience for this," he kissed her when she exited the car. "I will visit my mom; call me when you are ready."

He drove off, leaving her standing in Noreen Greystone's driveway. The house was painted in white and had a classic, timeless quality. The house's exterior had ivy completely covering one side and gorgeous purple roses in clusters near the entrance. Their scent was especially strong the closer you advanced to the front door.

Cinnamon stopped and took a deep breath. She closed her eyes and inhaled again. Now, she wished she could bottle and inhale this to uplift her spirit whenever she felt down.

"It's called Ebb Tide," Noreen said to her left; she was in full gardening gear, a broad hat, and gloves. "Today is my gardening day," she smiled at Cinnamon.

"Oh," Cinnamon smiled.

"But I was so intrigued to hear what you learned from the ladies in your family. We can recline on the patio if you just walk this way. Have you eaten?"

"No," Cinnamon said, "I have been too keyed up to eat."

"Well then, we can share lunch together," Noreen smiled. "The cook made Saturday soup, and I have garlic bread, fresh and warm from the oven."

Noreen led Cinnamon towards the inviting patio. There

was a gentle breeze and the distant sound of birdsong, which added to the serene ambiance of the place. They settled into comfortable recliners with plush cushions, and Noreen poured fragrant herbal tea into delicate cups. The patio overlooked a breathtaking view of the rolling hills, creating a picturesque backdrop for their conversation.

"Now, my dear," Noreen began, "tell me your story, and I will tell you mine."

Cinnamon took a moment to savor the aroma of the tea before delving into what she had heard. Noreen listened with rapt attention, nodding knowingly at some parts and frowning heavily at others.

"Rosemary is wrong," Noreen said, "you are indeed Ronald's child. Apparently, Richard did a DNA test with you and my mother when you were a toddler years ago; the results are in his documents if you want to see it."

Cinnamon nodded.

"Apparently, my mother knew about this too," Noreen sighed. "She swore Richard to secrecy; she didn't want her only son to be known as a pedophile, and she reasoned that he had already killed himself, so there was no need to rehash things. My mother is dead now, and so is Richard, so he felt free to at least leave me with the truth."

Cinnamon shook her head. There were secrets all around.

"Yes," Noreen said, "I learned a lot from the video that Richard left for me. I, like you, feel as if I was blindsided."

Cinnamon touched her hand across the table. "I am sorry."

"No child," Noreen squeezed her hand in hers, "I am the one who is sorry. You are my niece, but it came about at a steep price to your mother. Since that video that Richard sent, I feel like wrapping my arms around Anise and begging her forgiveness. We all failed her: Richard because she was the result of a secret affair, your mother because she turned a blind eye to what was going on, and my brother. I don't know how he became that way, but you are here, and despite the journey, you are the result. I am hoping we can forge a relationship from here."

"I'd like that," Cinnamon nodded.

Chapter Sixteen

It was a whirlwind leading up to the Greystones wine launch. Noreen had personally invited Anise and begged her to attend. Cinnamon and Cayenne were going separately. Sage unfortunately had exams and couldn't make it.

Cayenne was taking her girlfriend Alex, who had never been to anything so fancy.

Alex squealed. "This beats the perfume launch for Devina Shae that you took Cinnamon to instead of me. I can't believe you are related to Richard Greystone, and he is your grandfather."

Cayenne walked from her room, holding up two pairs of shoes. She wore a black dress, which emphasized her shape, and her hair was in a curly top knot. She looked really pretty. "Which one, Cinna?"

"They look the same," Cinnamon said.

"No, they are not. This one has glitter, and this one doesn't."

Cinnamon chuckled. "The one with glitter will match your dress."

"Thanks," Cayenne smiled, "by the way, you look hot.

Cinnamon laughed. "I was thinking the same about you. Don't be late, Jax is downstairs. See you later."

"You look stunning," Jax said when he pulled up at Cinnamon's place, and she opened the door. "Wow."

Cinnamon smiled. "Thank you. You look great, too. It's my first time seeing you in a tux."

Jax smiled.

"I feel a little nervous about tonight," Cinnamon sighed.

"I'll be around," Jax said reassuringly.

"What do you think Richard Greystone said in his video?"

"I don't have a clue," Jax said. "Maybe it would be a welcome for Anise to the family and a public acknowledgment of her."

Cinnamon nodded.

The courtyard at the Greystone Vineyard was simply stunning. It was decorated for the event with thousands of twinkling lights. Tables adorned with elegant white linens and flickering candles were strategically placed, creating an enchanting atmosphere beneath the starlit sky. A live band played jazz melodies in one corner, adding a harmonious backdrop to the festivities.

The scent of blooming flowers added a delicate touch to the air, and the gentle hum of conversations and laughter echoed through the courtyard.

"This is breathtaking, Jax. It's like stepping into a fairytale," she said, the awe heavy in her voice.

Jax smiled. "They went all out."

Leo approached with a glass of Rosemary Ruby in hand. "What do you think of the setup?"

"It's great!" Jax said.

"I love it," Cinnamon said.

"Your mother is here," Leo said to Cinnamon, "I don't know what grandma said to her, but they've been chummy ever since she arrived."

Anise was indeed there in a floor-length green dress, minimal makeup, and her hair in a bell around her face. She was, of course, the center of attention, chatting and laughing as if she had always been a part of that crowd.

"What's the name of this new wine?" Cinnamon asked.

"Jax didn't tell you?" Leo smiled.

"I forgot to ask," Cinnamon said.

"I would tell you to wait for the big reveal then, but the name of the wine is Anise Crystal. It was developed years ago, and this year he perfected it."

Leo was called away, and Cinnamon hooked her hand in Jax's.

"Are you okay?" He pulled her closer.

"Quite fine," Cinnamon said. "I think my mother needed this."

The surrealness of the night didn't change. Before the big reveal of the wine, Richard Greystone came on the screen.

"Goodnight, everyone. If you are watching me pre-taped, this means that I am not around. In a way, I am happy that I don't have to deal with the fallout surrounding the reveal of this this secret. I apologize to my sons and their children for having to deal with this, but some secrets are meant to be told. Not all, just some.

"And this one, I have wanted to share for decades. Anise Crystal is my daughter. I have always regretted keeping this particular secret. She deserves to be acknowledged and her rightful place be in the Greystone family.

"I have rectified that by giving her equal parts of my fortune and shares in the company as her brothers. Anise has had a tough life because of my neglect, and I will be eternally sorry for my hand in that.

"As you know, my wines tell a story, and this latest one, my Anise Crystal, describes my daughter perfectly. Like the person, the wine is complex, with layers that unfold gracefully over time. It carries a hint of resilience, much like Anise herself, who navigated life's challenges with strength and grace. The wine is bold yet subtle, just like the quiet determination that has defined her journey.

"Anise Crystal, like the woman it is named after, is a blend of sweetness and depth, capturing the essence of a well-lived life. It has the warmth of family, the richness of experience, and the promise of new beginnings. I hope that as you savor this vintage, you will enjoy the flavors and appreciate the story it tells—the story of a daughter finally acknowledged and embraced.

"To Anise, my sincere apologies for the years of silence. You are an integral part of the Greystone family, and your presence enriches us all. May this revelation bring healing, understanding, and a renewed sense of belonging.

"To my sons, thank you for your understanding and support during this unveiling. Family is a tapestry woven with both joy and challenges, and it's in our shared stories that we find the true meaning of unity.

"As I step away, I leave with a lighter heart for sharing this long-held secret. May the future of Greystone be as robust and enduring as the wines that bear its name.

"Goodnight and may each glass of Anise Crystal be a toast to new beginnings and the enduring power of family."

There were tears in Cinnamon's eyes when the video faded to black.

"That's so sweet," she whispered to Jax.

There was a crush of people around Anise as she basked

in her new found acceptance.

Chapter Seventeen

"Do you want to go home?" Jax asked when they were on their way home for what had turned out to be a fabulous party. "Or do you want to spend the night with me?"

"Stay with you," Cinnamon whispered.

They headed up to the penthouse floor in silence.

"Do you want to talk about it?" Jax asked.

"No," Cinnamon shook her head. "I just want you to kiss me and don't stop."

"Okay," Jax whispered, pulling her closer.

He kissed her gently on the lips. "I love you, Cinnamon Jade Cooper."

Cinnamon looked into Jax's eyes, her heart swelling with emotion. "I love you too, Jax Orion Wilde."

Jax smiled in relief. "Good."

He kissed her on her ear, and shivers ran up her spine.

"I have been carrying around a pack of flavored condoms," Cinnamon said. "My mother gave them to me for my birthday."

Jax chuckled. "We'll find use for them."

He led her to the bedroom and closed the door behind them. The soft glow of city lights filtered through the large windows, casting a warm ambiance in the room. Jax turned to Cinnamon, his eyes filled with affection.

"I'm glad you're here with me," Jax said, his voice low and intimate.

Cinnamon smiled, feeling a mixture of excitement and comfort. "Me too," she replied, her fingers tracing a gentle path along Jax's chest.

As they stood there, the atmosphere between them shifted, and the air was charged with anticipation.

Jax leaned in to kiss Cinnamon again, their connection deepening. The passion between them grew, and soon, they found themselves lost in each other.

Hours passed as they explored the depths of their emotions and desires. The world outside the penthouse seemed to fade away, leaving only the two of them wrapped up in the warmth of their love. Cinnamon and Jax navigated the night with laughter, whispers, and shared secrets, creating a bond that went beyond the physical.

In the quiet moments that followed, as they lay tangled in each other's arms, Cinnamon felt a sense of contentment she had never known before. Jax gently brushed a strand of hair from her face, his gaze tender.

"I'm glad you're in my life, Cinnamon," Jax said, his words filled with sincerity.

"Me too, Jax," Cinnamon replied, her heart brimming with happiness. "I never want this moment to end."

"It doesn't have to. We can spend all weekend together and, better yet, the rest of our lives."

Epilogue

Eighteen months later…

It was Jax and Cinnamon's baby shower; they had just found out they would have a boy. All the family had gathered in Noreen's backyard. Blue and silver streamers and balloons were everywhere, creating a convivial atmosphere. Jax was hogging the karaoke machine, dedicating all his songs to Cinnamon, who dutifully blew him kisses after every rendition.

"If I were a carpenter and you were a lady, would you marry me anyway? Would you have my baby?" Jax sang.

"Sure, honey," Cinnamon said, "I would marry you again and again and have your baby, of course." She cupped the large mound in front of her. "I can't wait to have your baby; this boy is resting on my bladder."

Cayenne sat beside her and grinned. "You have me to thank for meeting him, you know. If you hadn't come to that perfume launch, you wouldn't be here, happy and content."

"I know," Cinnamon smiled. "Thank you."

"I see you invited Nana Rosie," Cayenne said, "she and mom are conspicuously avoiding each other."

"I don't know what the latest flare-up is. Nana Rosie apologized for not believing her when she was a child; they both went to counseling and are doing much better." Cinnamon shrugged. "It's always something with them."

"You should put them beside each other in the family picture." Cayenne giggled. "Let them hug it out."

"I don't want to risk a quarrel," Cinnamon said, "the day has been going so well. Don't distract me. Jax is singing my favorite line from the song."

Cayenne smiled.

Jax belted out, see my love through loneliness, see my love through sorrow, I'm giving you my onliness...Come give me your tomorrow…

"That's my man," Cinnamon chuckled, rocking as he sang. "He sounds so good."

Cayenne nodded. "He does sound great."

They clapped when Jax finished his song.

Anise took the mic from him. "We get it, Jax, you love your wife."

Everyone around them laughed.

Jax came over, sat close, and kissed her. "Did you like that last song?"

"Loved it," Cinnamon caressed his face and looked at him lovingly.

"Ladies and gentlemen, family and friends," Anise said, "as many of you may know, I have been slowly dabbling in the wine business. In other words, I show up at the office daily and learn stuff. In exchange for my dedication, my nephew Leo has graciously offered that I develop and name the next wine in the Spice and Stone series.

"I wracked my brain trying to come up with an acceptable spice and stone wine that would knock the socks off of everyone. I went to the lab and tried different formulas, but nothing spoke to me.

"Then, lo and behold, Cinnamon became pregnant and found out it was a boy, and I thought how novel it would be for me to name the next wine in honor of my grandson.

"Now, I must say, when I first ran the idea by Cinnamon, she was not excited about it, but she made me promise to take my ADHD meds for six months first, never missing a day."

"I haven't missed a day," Anise continued.

Cinnamon groaned. "Good god, what did I get myself into?"

Jax chuckled. "It's a spice and a stone; how bad can it be?"

"Our child could be called Chili Gold," Cinnamon muttered, "or Mustard Topaz. Can you imagine the children in his class calling him Musty Top. Come here Musty Top!"

Jax chuckled.

Anise raised her glass, a glint of pride in her eyes, "I put a lot of thought and a lot of tasting into this, ladies and gentlemen, family and friends. As a matter of fact, what is in your glasses is a sample of my earnest efforts."

Jax took a sip of his wine and closed his eyes. "It is good."

"Excellent." Cayenne added.

"I wish I could taste it," Cinnamon said, "what is jumping out at you?"

"It may very well be better than Rosemary Ruby," Jax took another sip. "Anise has talent. She may be better than Richard."

Anise overheard and smiled.

"So let's raise our glasses to the newest addition to

our family and to a new chapter in the Greystone wine collection—Valerian Jett."

The crowd erupted in applause.

"VJ for short," Jax chuckled.

Cinnamon smiled. "Well, that's not bad…"

Jax gave her a reassuring squeeze. "It's good. Very good. Told you it couldn't be that bad. In fact, it has a nice buzz to it—Valerian Jett Wilde. I love it," he whispered with a grin. "And I love you."

"I love you too," Cinnamon smiled. "Now and forever."

Dear Reader,

THANK YOU for reading Cinnamon! If you enjoyed reading this book, PLEASE consider leaving a review.

If you have comments or suggestions, I welcome them. You can reach me and receive a reply at brenalbar@gmail.com.

Continue reading for an excerpt from Cayenne, the second book in the series.

Thanks again. All the best,

Happy Reading,

Brenda

Excerpt- Cayenne
(Book Two, Spice and Stone Series)

"I never thought I'd say this," Alex said, plopping herself down on the lounge chair beside Cayenne, "but I am in love."

Cayenne snorted. "You say it all the time." She was sipping a welcome drink brought to them by the butler at their villa.

"But this time, I really mean it," Alex said, "I swear from the moment Dirk walked into the office two months ago, my heart hasn't righted itself. Did I describe him to you?"

"Several times," Cayenne said patiently. She felt lightweight and carefree and could listen to Alex wax poetic all day about her coworker.

The breeze was refreshing, the scenery top-tier. Everywhere she looked, were blue skies and sea views.

Alex had rented an eight-bedroom villa for the long holiday weekend and had invited a few of her friends and this Dirk fellow, who she was constantly fawning over like a ditzy schoolgirl.

They had found the poolside after they had chosen their rooms and since then Dirk was all Alex could talk about.

"He has the aesthetic that I like," Alex said, "mocha-toned skin, thick level brows, dark brown eyes the color of rich mahogany, and juicy pink lips. I can barely concentrate on what he is saying most of the time. When he speaks, a rush of wind starts in my ear, and I only hear him from a distance. I see his lips though; they move in slow motion."

"Isn't that a bad thing?" Cayenne asked, concerned. "You just got promoted; you can't afford to zone out of hearing your colleagues, no matter how delicious they look."

"I know," Alex said, unconcerned. "But yet, I do it."

Cayenne adjusted her sunglasses and placed them on top of her hair. No matter how much Alex promoted Dirk, Cayenne didn't like him already. He wasn't a part of their friend crowd; Alex had asked him to stay for the whole weekend, and they didn't even know him. He would be a cuckoo in the group of twelve, changing the dynamic because Alex would act coquettish and coy around him. Cayenne hated it when Alex went into her sophisticated mode.

It would all be an act for the rest of their time there.

"What time is Dirk coming by?" Cayenne asked lazily.

"Why, you can't wait to meet him?"

"No," Cayenne said, "just wondering when you will start putting on your actress persona and start acting weird. As you do around every guy you like at first."

"I don't act weird," Alex sighed, "I do, don't I?"

"Oh yes," Cayenne nodded. "And when the thrill wears off, you start acting normal again, and then you get bored and dump them."

"I don't think I will ever be bored of Dirk James," Alex said dreamily. "When he stepped into the office on his first day, I instantly knew he would change my life. Do you think he'll like it here?"

"Oh, he will," Cayenne nodded. "It's gorgeous, luxurious, and exclusive. What's not to like? You are going all out for this weekend; it must be costing you an arm and a leg."

"It's fine," Alex said breezily.

"I didn't want to say anything," Cayenne said, concerned, "but you've been spending money recklessly lately. What about saving up for a house?"

"Relax, young one," Alex laughed, "I know what I am doing. I am the newest senior wealth manager at LAD Wealth Management. I should advise you on money management, not vice versa."

"I know," Cayenne said, "that is why I am concerned. I know how much you earn, and I know funding your latest lifestyle is not sustainable."

"You know about my base salary," Alex said, "but there are incentives and..." Her phone buzzed. Someone was at the gate.

She grabbed the phone and gasped. "He is here. He is not supposed to be here until twelve like the others."

"I have to go and get dressed," Alex said, panicking, "you go and greet him. Keep him entertained."

"Okay," Cayenne said, looking down at herself. She and Alex had on identical dresses. They were cute and lightweight. Cayenne had picked them up at a craft market. She felt peeved that Alex thought the dresses were not presentable enough for her precious Dirk.

"There is nothing wrong with your dress," she pointed to Alex, but her friend was already inside, running towards her room in a panic.

Cayenne shook her head. She didn't want to move from her sheltered spot overlooking the glistening blue pool, but she had to meet Dirk and keep him entertained per Alex's instructions.

She checked herself in the floor-to-ceiling mirror in the hallway and confirmed that there was nothing wrong with the dress. Her face was okay; she had chewed off all her lip gloss. She refreshed that and headed downstairs; when she opened the door, she fixed a welcoming smile.

"Hello there, Dirk," her voice faded as she stared at the man before her. She was shocked on so many levels. This guy before her was not Dirk James; he was Lance Cauldwell, her first love. She knew every line of that face. She had once tried to count every one of his thick, stubby eyelashes.

He looked the same, no better, way better. She saw why

Alex was gushing over him; she had done the same in the past, when she was seventeen and he was their next-door neighbor studying for his master's at the university.

"Lance!" Cayenne hissed, "When did you change your name to Dirk?"

"Excuse me?" the guy in front of her took a step back. He looked at her with no recognition behind his eyes. "It seems as if I have the wrong address!"

"No er…sorry," Cayenne stammered. She was confused. Was he Lance Cauldwell's twin or something? He obviously did not know who she was.

"My name is Cayenne," she cleared her throat, "Alex sent me to greet you; she went to freshen up."

"Oh, nice to meet you Cayenne," he held his hand out for her to shake and when Cayenne put her hand in his all the hairs on her arm stood on end.

She hurriedly pulled her hand away and stepped aside for him to pass.

She had only had this reaction to one guy, his name was Lance Cauldwell and he looked exactly like Dirk James. Something was not adding up for her here.

Discover Exclusive Offers and Be the First to Know!

If you haven't already, don't miss out on the opportunity to join my New Release Newsletter! Sign up today and become part of an exclusive community where you'll be among the first to hear about my latest book releases and take advantage of special prices.

Why join my mailing list?

Be the First: Get a head start and be the first to know when I release a new book.

Exclusive Discounts: Unlock special prices available only to subscribers. Enjoy limited time offers and save big on your favorite books.

Quick and Easy: Signing up takes less than 30 seconds.

To join, visit https://www.brenalbar.com/newsletter or scan the QR code below.

Thank you for your support, and happy reading!

Ridgeview Series

The Ridgeview series follows five couples on the Jamaican north coast in the luxurious community of Ridgeview. It explores their everyday struggles with careers, children, and family drama. Each book touches on love, marriage, and trust as the characters face challenges that test their relationships.

Ride or Die (Book 1)
Play For Keeps (Book 2)
Through Thick and Thin (Book 3)
Tried and True (Book 4)
Stay With You (Book 5)

Spice and Stone Series

Join three extraordinary girls—Cinnamon, Cayenne, and Sage—as they navigate the intricate flavors of life, love, and romance in the captivating Spice and Stone series.

Cinnamon (Book 1)
Cayenne (Book 2)
Sage (Book3)

The Crimson Hill Series

Where family drama, romance, and a touch of sci-fi blend seamlessly in the enchanting backdrop of a small town in Jamaica. Prepare to embark on an unforgettable journey as secrets unravel, passions ignite, and destinies intertwine.

No Goodbye (Book 1)
No Misunderstanding (Book 2)
No Ordinary Love (Book 3)
No Fairy Tale (Book 4)
No Letting Go (Book 5)
No Strings Attached (Book 6)
No More Mrs. Nice Girl (Book 7)
No Place Like You (Book 8)
Knight and Day (Book 8.5)
No Expectations (Book 9)
Ice and Fyre (Book 9.5)
No Surrender (Book 10)
No Time for Love (Book 11)
No Promises (Book 12)
Winter's Eve (Book 13)

The Wiley Brothers

Step into the world of the Wiley Brothers, where tragedy weaves an unbreakable bond and love becomes their guiding light. In this captivating series, follow the journey of six remarkable boys as they navigate the tumultuous path of growing up without parents, discovering love, and finding their place in a challenging world.

Between Brothers (Book 0)- How it all began…
For Pete's Sake (Book 1)- Preston's story.
Crossing Jordan (Book 2)-Jordan's story.
Fire and Walter (Book 3)- Walter's story.
The Perfect Guy (Book 4)-Guy's Story.
The Patience of a Saint (Book 5)- Saint's Story.
A Case of Love (Book 6)- Case's Story.

The Pryce Sisters

Follow the remarkable journey of the Pryce triplets as they navigate the complexities of growing up, discovering romance, and embracing the exhilarating challenges of the new adult years.

Baby For A Pryce- Book 1
Right Pryce Wrong Time – Book 2
Yours, For A Pryce- Book 3

The Jacksons

Prepare to be enthralled by the captivating saga of the Jackson family. In this gripping series, secrets unravel, paternity questions loom, and love blooms in the most unexpected corners.

Ace- Book 1
Deuce- Book 2
Trey- Book 3
Quade- Book 4

The Scarlett Series

Their patriarch died and unexpectedly left each of them a fortune. Watch as the Scarlett family navigate their way through the ups and downs of sudden wealth, family secrets, and the complicated dynamics of their relationships.

Scarlett Baby (Book 1)
Scarlett Sinner (Book 2)
Scarlett Secret (Book 3)
Scarlett Love (Book 4)
Scarlett Promise (Book 5)
Scarlett Bride (Book 6)
Scarlett Heart (Book 7)

Magnolia Sisters

They were the rejects. The worst of the lot, they grew up in a girl's home together and formed sisterly bonds. Each book in the series tells the story of a different girl and the unique struggles and triumphs she faces along the way. With themes of friendship, forgiveness, and the power of love, the "Magnolia Sisters" series is a heartwarming and inspiring read that you won't want to put down.

Dear Mystery Guy- Book 1
Bad Girl Blues- Book 2
Her Mistaken Dream- Book 3
Just Like Yesterday – Book 4

New Song Series

A group of friends started out as a church band, see how each of them navigate their personal and professional lives while staying true to their faith and facing challenges along the way. With themes of forgiveness, redemption, and second chances, the New Song Series is a captivating read for anyone who enjoys heartwarming stories of love and faith.

Going Solo- Book 1
Duet on Fire- Book 2
Tangled Chords- Book 3
Broken Harmony- Book 4
A Past Refrain- Book 5
Perfect Melody- Book 6

The Bancrofts

The Bancroft family delves into the inner workings of academia and the high-stakes world of university politics. The family wrestles with the pressures of maintaining their family's legacy, they must confront their own demons and navigate the complex relationships that bind them together. From unexpected love affairs and betrayals to scandals and secrets that threaten to tear them apart, this is a series that will keep you captivated until the very end.

Homely Girl- Book 0
Saving Facc- Book 1
Tattered Tiara- Book 2
Private Dancer- Book 3
Goodbye Lonely- Book 4
Practice Run- Book 5
Sense of Rumor- Book 6
A Younger Man- Book 7
Just To See Her- Book 8

Three Rivers Series

Three Rivers Series, a captivating tale of love, redemption, and second chances set in a picturesque community in St. Ann's Bay, Jamaica.

Private Sins- Book 1
Loving Mr. Wright- Book 2
Unholy Matrimony- Book 3
If It Ain't Broke- Book 4

The Resetter Series

The Resetter Series takes a look at a rare kind of person, a person who can travel back in time, but they only have one chance to get things right if they go back! With themes of second chances, changing the past and the power of love, the resetters series is a captivating time travel romance that many readers have described as a page turner.

Never Too Late- Book 1
Never Say Never- Book 2
Now or Never- Book 3
Almost Never- Book 4

On the Rebound Series

Experience the gripping and emotionally charged On the Rebound series, where love, betrayal, and redemption collide in a whirlwind of passion and secrets. Brace yourself for a journey filled with drama, cheating scandals, DNA questions, and ultimately, the power of second chances and finding love again.

On the Rebound- Book 1
On the Rebound Book 2

Standalone Books

Full Circle- After graduating from university, Diana wanted to return to Jamaica to find her siblings. What she didn't foresee was that she would meet Robert Cassidy and that both their pasts would be intertwined, and that disturbing questions would pop up about their parentage just when they were getting close.

After the End- Torn between two lovers. Colleen married her high school sweetheart, Isaiah, hoping that they would live happily ever after, but life intruded, and Isaiah disappeared at sea. She found work with the rich and handsome Enrique Lopez as a housekeeper and realized that she couldn't keep him at arm's length.

Love Triangle: Three Sides to the Story- George, the husband. Marie, the wife, and Karen-the mistress. They all get to tell their side of the story.

New Beginnings- Inner-city girl Geneva was offered an opportunity of a lifetime when she learned that her 'real' father was a wealthy man. Her decision to live up-town meant she had to leave Froggie, her 'ghetto don,' behind. She also found herself battling with her stepmother and battling her emotions for Justin, a suave up-towner.

The Preacher and the Prostitute- Prostitution and the clergy don't mix. Tell that to ex-prostitute Maribel, who finds herself in love with the Pastor at her church. Can an ex-prostitute and a pastor have a future together?

Historical Fiction

You won't want to miss out on these two captivating reads!

"The Pull of Freedom" tells the story of a slave family and their desperate struggle for freedom in Jamaica's colonial era. Follow the journey of these brave individuals as they fight for their right to be free, facing danger, heartbreak, and unimaginable obstacles along the way.

"The Empty Hammock" takes readers on a journey through time, as a modern woman finds herself transported back to the Taino era of Jamaica's history. Experience the wonder and mystery of this ancient culture through her eyes, as she learns about their traditions, beliefs, and way of life. With richly drawn characters and a beautifully realized setting, "The Empty Hammock" is a must-read for anyone who loves historical fiction that transports them to another time and place.

Short Story Collections

Di Taxi Ride and Other Stories- Funny stories about Jamaican life to make you laugh.

www.ingramcontent.com/pod-product-compliance
Lightning Source LLC
Chambersburg PA
CBHW061302120726
48001CB00001B/430